Intermediate

★ 中級全民英檢必備
★ 學科能力測驗／指定科目考試／統一入學測驗必備

Intermediate Reading ②
完全閱讀導引

李文玲

學歷
國立高雄師範大學英語系
經歷
臺北市立中山女子高級中學
臺北市立第一女子高級中學英語教師

三民書局

國家圖書館出版品預行編目資料

Intermediate Reading 2 完全閱讀導引／李文玲編著.－
－初版五刷.－－臺北市：三民，2012
面；　公分

ISBN 978-957-14-4812-1　（平裝）

1.英國語言－讀本

805.18　　　　　　　　　　　　　　　96012280

ⓒ　Intermediate Reading 2 完全閱讀導引

編 著 者	李文玲
發 行 人	劉振強
著作財產權人	三民書局股份有限公司
發 行 所	三民書局股份有限公司
	地址　臺北市復興北路386號
	電話　(02)25006600
	郵撥帳號　0009998-5
門 市 部	(復北店)臺北市復興北路386號
	(重南店)臺北市重慶南路一段61號
出版日期	初版一刷　2007年7月
	初版五刷　2012年10月
編　　號	S 807050

行政院新聞局登記證局版臺業字第○二○○號

有著作權‧不准侵害

ISBN　978-957-14-4812-1　（平裝）

http://www.sanmin.com.tw　三民網路書店
※本書如有缺頁、破損或裝訂錯誤，請寄回本公司更換。

序

知識，就是希望；閱讀，就是力量。

在這個資訊爆炸的時代，應該如何選擇真正有用的資訊來吸收？
在考場如戰場的競爭壓力之下，應該如何儲備實力，漂亮地面對挑戰？
身為地球村的一份子，應該如何增進英語實力，與世界接軌？
學習英文的目的，就是要讓自己在這個資訊爆炸的時代之中，突破語言的藩籬，站在吸收新知的制高點之上，以閱讀獲得力量，以知識創造希望！

針對在英文閱讀中可能面對的挑戰，我們費心規劃 Reading Power 系列叢書，希望在學習英語的路上助您一臂之力，讓您輕鬆閱讀、快樂學習。
本系列叢書分為三個等級：
Basic：適用於大考中心公佈之詞彙分級表中第一、二級（前兩千個單字）的範圍；適用於全民英檢初級。
Intermediate：適用於大考中心公佈之詞彙分級表中第三、四級（第兩千到四千個單字）的範圍；適用於全民英檢中級。
Advanced：適用於大考中心公佈之詞彙分級表中第五、六級（第四千到七千個單字）的範圍；適用於全民英檢中高級。
我們希望以這樣的分級方式，讓讀者能針對自己的需求及程度選擇適合的書籍。

誠摯希望在學習英語的路上，這套 Reading Power 系列叢書將伴隨您找到閱讀的力量，發揮知識的光芒！

給讀者的話

　　本書設計的目的是希望以循序漸進的方式，引導讀者認識最基本的閱讀技巧，並逐步提升閱讀能力。而本書與其他閱讀訓練書籍最大的不同之處，是將內容區分為兩大部分，以「先了解理論，再進行實戰」的概念，讓讀者在閱讀這個區塊得到完整的啟發，然後再藉由文章與閱讀測驗題目達成大量練習的目標。現在我們分別介紹如下：

　　第一部份為 <理論篇>，目標是希望讀者在應付一篇三百字以內的文章和五個題目之前，能夠一步一步打好根基，學會各種題型 (question types) 所要運用的不同策略和技巧。這一部分先介紹 Skimming 和 Scanning 這兩項基本而重要的閱讀技巧，之後六個單元介紹大考中閱讀測驗最常出現的六種題型(主旨、細節、字義、類推、代名詞的指涉、作者的態度/目的和文章的調性)以及答題的技巧。在淺顯而精要的講解之後，每一單元還設計了小練習，依據循序漸進與由淺入深的原則設計，例如 Unit 3 字義題型和 Unit 4 類推題型都先由單句的練習開始，之後進入段落練習。

　　第二部份為 <測驗篇>，共有四十篇 250～300 字的文章，每篇文章之後附有五個問題。文章的主題十分多元化且能兼顧知識性與趣味性，題目也極具深度，完全涵蓋了第一部份的六種題型，期盼讀者可以將第一部份學到的技巧在此好好應用並且自我檢測。

　　這是一本引領你學習技巧，提升閱讀能力的書。希望能幫助你在閱讀的領域中更上層樓，在測驗中脫穎而出！

Acknowledgements:

The articles in this publication are adapted from the works by: Monideepa Banerjee, James Baron, Tara Benwell, Violaine Combet, Jason Crockett, Editage, Lani Evans, Sue Farley, Lee Price Fernon, Ian Fletcher, Quinn Genze, Paul Hsiung Go, Stephen Goodchild, Robert Gouthro, Jason Grenier, Toni Jordan, Carol Lauderdale, Karl Nilsson, Theodore Pigott, Rhishipal Ramachandran, Joseph E. Schier, Sharon Shreet, Justin Silves, Amelia Smolar, Han Tseng, Karen Le Vasseur, Melanie Votaw, Vanessa York, and Maria Zinovieva.

Table of Contents

理論篇

INTERMEDIATE READING 2

Unit 1 Skimming & Scanning

Skimming (略讀) 和 Scanning (查讀/尋讀)是閱讀最基本的技巧，學會這些技巧對閱讀速度和理解能力都有幫助。而且在做閱讀測驗題目時，好幾種題型都會運用到這兩種技巧。

運用的技巧 1 —— **Skimming**

Skimming (略讀)這個技巧可以幫你快速地抓住文章的主旨、大意、作者的觀點或立場。要訣是集中精神快速瀏覽，不需全盤閱讀，選擇性的略過一些部分，只需抓住重要(能讓你得知文章主旨大意)的部分，例如引言或主題句、每一段的前一兩句等，大約可以比正常閱讀速度快三、四倍。

試試看閱讀劃底線的部分然後回答問題：

From a physiological standpoint, plants are completely different from animals. Animals have central nervous systems and brains. They are able to feel pain so that they can use it for self-protection. For example, if you touch something hot and feel pain, you will learn from this discomfort that you should not touch that item in the future. On the other hand, plants cannot move from place to place and do not need to learn to avoid certain things, so this sensation would be unnecessary. Therefore, unlike animals' body parts, many fruits and vegetables can be harvested over and over again without dying. (改寫自 94 年度學測考題)

■(1) What does the passage mainly discuss?

_____

■(2) The passage was written mainly to _____.

(A) compare　(B) tell a story　(C) amuse the reader

Answer: (1) It discusses the physiological difference between plants and animals.

(2) A

Activities

1. 以下有五篇短文，請用略讀的技巧找出主旨，回答問題。

When we exercise, we burn more calories. Tests show that vigorous exercise that increases body temperature and makes us sweat will raise our metabolic rate. As a result, we continue burning extra calories for several hours even when we stop exercising. In addition, getting exercise causes food to pass through our intestinal tract much faster. So we absorb a decreased percentage of the food we take in. It is reported that a marathon runner has a food transit time of 4 to 6 hours, but an average person needs 24 hours for a meal to pass through. Finally, exercise also helps us lose weight by boosting our motivation to stick to our weight loss program.

■ _____ This passage mainly discusses about _____.

⒜ how exercise helps raise metabolic rate

⒝ why exercise helps burn calories

⒞ how exercise helps lose weight

2. 以略讀的技巧抓住重點，然後作答。

Evolutionary psychologists say that men see traits that show a woman's ability to bear and raise healthy children as beauty. In study after study, men have been found to be most attracted to women with certain characteristics. They prefer women with balanced facial features, soft unblemished skin, wide toothy smiles, shiny hair, and shapely figures. Lovely skin, teeth, and hair indicate that a woman has enjoyed good health and adequate nutrition throughout her lifetime. And a shapely figure hints at fitness for childbirth.

■ _____ What would be the best title for this passage?

⒜ The Importance of Women's Health

⒝ What is Beauty in Men's Eyes?

⒞ Women's Ability to Bear and Raise Children

3. 以下是新聞報導，以略讀的技巧抓住重點，然後作答。

A 10-year-old girl, Su-mei, was killed in a weekend blaze. The fire also took the life of her 3-year-old brother, Da-jin.

Her another brother, Da-nian, 7, was badly burned in their home in Miau-li. He is now receiving careful treatment at Burn Center in the Miau-li Hospital.

The raging fire early Saturday morning was probably caused by a heater which was too close to blankets. The three children were left home by their parents and were unable to find a key to open their apartment's double-locked doors.

■ _____ The news story is about _____.

⒜ a policeman on duty

⒝ a weekend fire

⒞ a weekend trip

4. 以下這篇文章，略去不重要的細節，只保留 Introduction、Conclusion 和每一段第一句。快速瀏覽這些文字，然後作答(限四十秒)。

Alexandria, the second largest city and the main port of Egypt, is the country's major summer resort. It is 225 kilometers northwest from Cairo on the Mediterranean. Its charming beaches, lively atmosphere, and ancient remains attract countless tourists.

In 332 B.C., Alexander the Great, its founder, conquered Egypt....

In 30 B.C., the city formally became part of the Roman Empire, and was the greatest of the Roman provincial capitals....

The city fell to the Arabs in 642 and its decline continued....

Napoleon took the city in 1789, but it fell to the British in 1801....

The city regained importance after the Mahmudiya Canal was completed in 1819....

Today, Alexandria has a population of about 3 million people and is Egypt's most important harbor on the Mediterranean. Its Mediterranean ambiance and cultural heritage make it different from the rest cities of the country. No trip would be complete without a visit to this fascinating city.

■ _____ (1) The article is about _____ .

(A) a summer resort in Egypt

(B) a city in Europe

(C) a story of Alexander the Great

(D) the Mediterranean

■ _____ (2) The author tells us about Alexandria's geographical information, special atmosphere, and _____ .

(A) beautiful residential sections

(B) ecological environment

(C) historical background

5. 以下是一篇完整的文章，運用略讀的技巧閱讀，然後作答(限四十秒)。

The best solar cells in the world are found in plants, which easily turn sunlight into the energy they need for growth. Recently, a scientist has discovered a way to use the light-catching proteins in spinach to make sunlight into electricity.

These spinach proteins are called Photosystem I. For many years, however, no one could find a way to make the proteins work with electronic items. Proteins need water and salt, but water and salt do not work well with electronics. Fortunately, a scientist has created a special shell that protects the proteins. The shell keeps water inside the shell and prevents it from leaking out. In other words, these shells not only allow Photosystem I proteins to remain wet, but also prevent water from touching electric parts.

To test this invention, the scientist put a piece of glass with a material that conducted electricity in the special shells. A semiconductor with an electrode was placed below. When light was shone on the piece of glass, the spinach proteins collected this energy and passed it along to the semiconductor and the electrode. Even though the electric current produced was not that strong, the experiment was a success.

Perhaps some day, special solar cells that use plant proteins might be used to extend battery life in cell phones or laptop computers.

_____ (1) What's the main idea of this article?

   (A) Scientists have found that the best solar cells use plant proteins.

   (B) Scientists are trying to use spinach proteins to make electricity.

   (C) A special shell has been made to protect plant proteins.

_____ (2) This article most likely appears in a _____ .

   (A) cookbook   (B) book review   (C) science magazine

運用的技巧 2 —— Scanning

Scanning (查讀/尋讀) 這技巧可以幫助你在一大篇文字或資料中,快速地找到你的目標。心中牢記你要找的關鍵字,一目數行地快速搜尋、掃視資料、找到關鍵字。這技巧也經常運用在日常生活中,例如:查字典、搜尋網頁、查看報紙的電影放映時間或電視節目表、查目錄或時刻表等等。

先在題目中找到關鍵字,再以查讀的技巧在文章中搜尋該關鍵字,找到答案。

■ _____The Indians respected the wolf because it _____.

   (A) was good at hunting

   (B) was good at disguising

   (C) had beautiful skins and paws

   (D) was an enemy to the white man

Native Americans could not understand the white man's war on the wolf. The Lakoa, Blackfeet, and Shoshone, among other tribes, considered the wolf their spiritual brother. They respected the animals' endurance and hunting ability, and warriors prayed to hunt like them. They draped themselves in wolf skins and paws, hoping they could acquire the wolf's hunting skills of stealth, courage, and stamina. Plains Indians wore wolf-skin disguises on raiding parties. Elite Comanche warriors were called wolves. （取自 95 年度指考考題）

Tip: 1. 這個題目的關鍵字是 respected。

2. 在文章中找到 "They respected the animals endurance and hunting ability, and warriors prayed to hunt like them.",瞭解句意之後知道答案就是 A。

Activities

1. 這是旅遊的行程資料，記住答題順序：一個題目→查讀→回答一個問題。

   (1) In which city will you visit the Bridge of Sighs?

   (2) In which city will you visit the Sistine Chapel?

   (3) In which city will you visit Juliet's Balcony?

   (4) How many cities will you visit?

   (5) In which city will you be given time for shopping?

Italian Holiday

- *Round trip scheduled air transportation*
- *12 Meals (5 dinners and 7 breakfasts)*
- *Venice—Canal cruise seeing St. Mark's Square, Doge's Palace and the Bridge of Sighs*
- *Verona, the city of Shakespeare's Romeo and Juliet*
- *Florence—See the marble cathedral Duomo, Ponte Vecchio Bridge and time to shop*
- *Siena, Italian capital of the Middle Ages*
- *Assisi—See the Basilica of St. Francis*
- *Ancient Rome—See the Colosseum, Circus Maximus, Forum and Trevi Fountain*
- *Vatican City—St. Peter's Basilica and the Sistine Chapel*

---

2. 這是四個景點的資料，記住答題順序：一個題目→查讀→回答一個問題。

   (1) Which park is the largest?

   (2) Which park offers activities for the whole family, including the old members?

(3) Which park provides an area for dogs running?

(4) Which park has a beach where you can do sunbathing?

(5) In which park can you test your ice-skating skills?

(6) Which park has a water-play area for kids?

Green Park

The park attracts many visitors for its 70 trailer and 200 tent campsites set among 400 acres. Hikers will enjoy wandering through about 8.3 miles of trails within the campsite and the picnic areas. Beach-goers will also enjoy our beautiful beach, having a peaceful day of sunbathing and swimming.

Sherwood Park

The 100-acre park provides young people with several sports and play areas. Our swimming complex includes an Olympic-size pool, a diving pool, a training pool, a kiddie pool, and a water-play area. The playground has areas for children of all age groups. Children's eyes will light up when they see the park's indoor artificial ice-skating rink.

Davon Park

Everyone can find something to do in our 235-acre park, which offers every type of sport, from handball to roller skating. There are 6 handball courts, six tennis courts, two basketball courts, three soccer fields. Even pets can enjoy a happy afternoon in an area for dogs to run.

Chesterfield Park

The 82-acre park offers activities for the whole family. For visitors who like to swim, we have an Olympic-size pool, a waterslide and a kiddie pool. Several athletic fields, including baseball and football fields, are lighted for night play with a permit. For senior citizens who need a little relaxation, we have a quiet area with chess and checker tables.

3. 這是一則簡短的新聞，記住答題順序：一個題目→查讀→回答一個問題。

(1) What is the official slogan?

(2) When did the slogan begin to appear on all license plates?

(3) Who signed the bill?

> Illinois celebrated its golden anniversary as "the Land of Lincoln" on Tuesday. On May 17, 1995, former governor William Stratton signed a bill into a law officially recognizing Abraham Lincoln as the state's favorite son. In the same year, the official slogan began to appear on all license plates and many state-produced items.

4. 運用查讀的技巧閱讀以下段落，並回答問題。

(1)_____ How many activities are mentioned in this passage?

(A) Three.　(B) Four.　(C) Five.

(2)_____ Which of the following activities is NOT mentioned in this passage?

(A) Hunting.　(B) Camping.　(C) Surfing.

　　Although Grants Pass, Oregon, is a fairly small town, it offers much to amuse summer visitors. Visitors can go rafting down the Rogue River or swimming in the Applegate River. Fishing in the area is another popular activity. Lots of people also go hunting for wild berries that grow along the roadsides. In addition, there are lovely clean campgrounds where campers can park their vehicles.

(取自 84 年度推甄考題)

5. 運用查讀的技巧閱讀以下段落，並回答問題。

(1)_____ The new type of the restaurant created by the McDonald brothers attracted people because of its _____.

(A) fancy menus and high sales   (B) fast service and low prices

(C) high prices and efficient service

(2)_____ What did Ray Kroc intend to sell when he visited the brothers in 1954?

(A) Burgers.   (B) Frying pans.   (C) Milkshake mixers.

(3)_____ When did Ray Kroc eventually buy the McDonald's?

(A) In 1954.   (B) In 1960.   (C) In 1964.

The McDonald brothers created a new kind of restaurant in the 1940s. They wanted fast service, low prices and high sales. They had a simple menu and designed a factory-like kitchen where trained staff could produce meals, like workers on an assembly line. People were attracted by the efficient service and soon the brothers opened more restaurants. They also started franchising, allowing other businessmen to open restaurants with the McDonald's name and standard operating procedures. In exchange, the brothers were paid a small percentage of the sales.

In 1954, Ray Kroc, a salesman, visited the McDonald brothers' restaurant in San Bernadino, California with the intention of selling them his milkshake mixers. When he saw the long but fast-moving line of customers buying burgers and fries, he thought to himself, "This will go anyplace!" He made a deal with the brothers and persuaded them to expand nationwide by putting him in control of franchising. "Anyplace" was a worldwide dream for Kroc, but not for the McDonald brothers. They were happy to sell him the company in 1960. In 1966, Kroc listed the company on the New York Stock Exchange to attract money for international expansion, beginning in Canada (1967). By the time he died in 1984, McDonald's was opening a restaurant somewhere in the world every seventeen hours!

Answer & Tip

★ **Skimming**

1. C   2. B   3. B   4.(1) A (2) C   5.(1) B (2) C

解析

1. 由承轉語 in addition 和 finally 可以找到三項要點，得知此段落談運動可以幫助減重。

2. 段落主題句(第一句)中可以找到答案。

3. 由第一段兩個句子就可以知道是一場週末火災。

4.(1) 第一段的第一句中可以得知答案。

 (2) 由第一段最後一句中的 ancient remains「古代遺跡」，可以得知是歷史背景。

5.(1) 第一段第二句即為本文主旨。

 (2) 主旨很清楚地顯示本文是科學性的文章。

★ **Scanning**

1.(1) Venice.   (2) Vatican City.   (3) Verona.   (4) Seven cities.

 (5) Florence.

2.(1) Green Park.   (2) Chesterfield Park.   (3) Davon Park.   (4) Green Park.

 (5) Sherwood Park.   (6) Sherwood Park.

3.(1) The Land of Lincoln.   (2) In 1995.   (3) William Stratton.

4.(1) C   (2) C

5.(1) B   (2) C   (3) B

解析

1. 抓住題目的關鍵字，就很容易可以在資料中找到答案。

2. 抓住題目的關鍵字到段落中快速搜尋，就可以找到答案。

3. (1) 抓住關鍵字 slogan「標語」，搜尋以大寫出現的字詞就是答案。

   (2)(3) 搜尋時間和人物的關鍵字。

4. 承轉語 or、another、also 和 in addition 可以提供答案的指引。

5. (1) 根據題目的 new type of restaurant， 在文章第一段找到 new kind of restaurant，下一句就是答案。

   (2) 在文章第二段找到關鍵字 Ray Kroc 和 selling，答案就在這一句。

   (3) 在文章第二段找到關鍵字 happy to sell 和 company，答案就在這一句。

Unit 2 Main Idea Questions

主旨 (main idea) 簡單來說就是文章的重點。這類題目測驗你是否掌握作者的中心思想，以及瞭解作者主要談些什麼。

✳ 一般的出題形式

1. What is the main idea of this passage?

2. This passage is/discusses mainly about _____ .

3. Which of the following would be the best title for this passage?

✳ 找尋主旨的方法

1. 如果是單一段落的文章，可以先找出主題句，因為作者會藉此句清楚地表達出文章主旨。主題句通常出現在段落的開頭或結尾。如果主題句表達得不夠完整，就要看看它的上一句或下一句，主旨有可能綜合了兩句的文意。

2. 如果是好幾個段落的文章，除了找到第一段引言的主題句之外，還要參考其他段落的主題句來掌握主旨。

3. 有時候作者不明說其主旨，而隱藏在段落或文章中，那就必須讀完全文才能清楚地瞭解主旨是什麼。

Activities

請選出以下各篇短文的主旨

1.　　The cat's ear is structured like a human being's: the inner ear, the middle ear, and the outer ear. The difference lies in the development of the inner ear. With supersensitive hearing, the cat is able to pick up sounds that are inaudible to us. Thanks to its ability to amplify sounds, the cat can hear the faintest noises.

　■ _____ What is the main idea of this passage?

　　　　(A) The structure of a cat's ear is very similar to that of a human being's.

(B) Like human beings, cats have supersensitive hearing, so they can hear the faintest noises.

(C) With powerful hearing, cats can hear the sounds that are too faint for humans to hear.

2.　　Even low-tech industries like the clothing industry benefit from nanotechnology. For example, several clothing manufacturers are using nanotechnology to make stain-resistant clothes. As this application and others spread throughout the clothing industry, the result will be clothes that last longer and never have to be ironed. You will also save money because you won't have to use dry-cleaners, or buy stain remover and detergent to keep your clothes clean and new-looking.

　　■_____What is the main idea of this passage?

　　　　(A) The use of nanotechnology makes clothes more resistant to water.

　　　　(B) With nanotechnology, people can save time and money on keeping clothes in a good condition.

　　　　(C) Nanotechnology brings a lot of benefits to clothing manufacturers.

3.　　Many legends regarding the origin of 1000 Island Dressing seem to relate back to George Boldt. While Boldt was cruising on the river among the 1000 Islands, Boldt's steward served a new dressing on the lunch salad. Boldt was pleased with its taste. He named it 1000 Island Dressing in honor of the beautiful area where it was first prepared.

　　■_____What would be the best title for this passage?

　　　　(A) How 1000 Island Dressing Was First Prepared.

　　　　(B) How 1000 Island Dressing Got Its Name.

　　　　(C) Cruising Among 1000 Islands is Fun.

4.   How can parents help children with their friendship? The most powerful influence we have on our children is not what we say but what we do. They are watching as we chat with neighbors across fences or in apartment stairwells. They are learning our values as we offer a cup of tea or help change a flat tire. They are trying to understand when we fail to reach out or when we turn away. Showing our children that friendships do matter—through our own friendships—is the most reliable strategy of all.

■ _____ What is the main idea of this passage?

(A) Showing children the importance of friendship is the best way to help them with friendship.

(B) What we say is more important than what we do when we educate our children.

(C) Helping our children with their friendship is the most reliable strategy to get close to them.

5.   Most people believe that forgiveness can only be good for the person who receives it. The forgiver is not really getting anything, and is even losing the chance to punish the other person. However, modern studies show that people who can forgive are healthier and happier than those who can't. In the United States, a study was made of a group who had been hurt by lovers, parents, friends or co-workers. Those who forgave the people that had wronged them were healthier than the ones who stayed angry and wouldn't forget their pain. The forgivers had lower blood pressure, fewer heart diseases and enjoyed better health. The non-forgivers had greater health problems and were more likely to become sick and die younger.

■ _____ What's the main idea of this passage?

(A) Forgiveness can only be good for the person who receives it.

(B) People who can forgive are healthier and happier than those who can't.

(C) The forgivers are always the people who enjoy better health.

6.   Ancient Egyptians believed a person was composed of the "ka," the spiritual element, and the "ba," the person's character. At the time of death, the two would separate and leave the body through the mouth of the dead person to begin a journey to the gods. After death, the ka and ba united to form the "akh," which would live in peace with the gods. That's why the Egyptians' dead bodies were preserved with their mouths open, leaving no obstruction of the path leading to the gods.

■_____ This passage discusses mainly about _____.

(A) how Egyptian spirits turned into gods

(B) how the "ka" and the "ba" untied to form "akh"

(C) why the mouths of Egyptians' dead bodies were kept wide open

7.   Extreme TV shows have become more and more popular. Some viewers love them because they never know what crazy stunt or outrageous action they will see next. They enjoy watching normal people do wild and unexpected things. Others say that these shows are entertaining and filled with more action than traditional action movies and TV shows.

■_____ The passage is mainly about _____.

(A) the crazy stunts in TV shows

(B) the reasons extreme shows become popular

(C) the traditional action movies

8.   Most of the UFO or alien reports come from honest people who are not trying to make money or become famous by reporting such sightings. However, non-believers think that they are merely imagining the sightings. No one really knows the truth, but there is an equal amount of evidence to support both sides.

There have been many cases of people faking alien findings. A good example is the "Hudson Valley Sightings." From 1982 to 1995, people from Hudson Valley, New York would regularly see a huge V-shaped UFO in the sky. This hoax was carried out by a group of pilots who flew their planes with lights tied together and formed a "V." Hundreds of people saw this and believed that they were seeing UFOs.

However, there are also some findings that are considered genuine. One of these is that of the archaeologist Chi Pu Tei. In 1938, he discovered a strange row of graves in the Baian Kara Ula mountains on the China-Tibet border. He found cave drawings of planets and of men wearing helmets as well as skeletons of small, delicate bodies with unnaturally large heads. Since this one took place at a time when technology was not advanced, it is considered a "real" finding as it could not have been artificially created.

Some evidence does suggest that aliens exist and that they have visited Earth. However, such findings can be easily faked. As a result, before people draw any conclusions based on reports of alien findings or sightings, it is important to make sure they are not hoaxes.

■ _____ What is the main idea of this passage?

(A) Some reports of alien sightings are hoaxes, but some evidence does show aliens have visited Earth.

(B) Advanced technology makes it possible to create UFO findings.

(C) Most of the reports of UFO sightings are unreliable.

Answer & Tip

1. C　　2. B　　3. B　　4. A　　5. B　　6. C　　7. B　　8. A

解析

1. 這是沒有主題句的段落，內容提到貓有非常敏銳的聽力，能聽到人無法聽到的細微聲音。

2. 這是主旨不明顯的段落，文中提到的重點是奈米技術使衣服不容易髒而且免燙，可以省去一些時間與費用。

3. 這是沒有主題句的段落，段落重點是千島醬的起源。

4. 主題句在最後一句：透過自己的友誼讓孩子知道朋友的重要是最可靠的方式。

5. 前兩句用來引入正題用，第三句以 however 引出主題句。

6. 由最後一句得知本段說明：埃及人死後的儀式中，屍體保持開口狀是為了讓通往神的道路暢通。

7. 第一句是主題句，支持句子都在說明理由。

8. 引言的第三句是主題論述句，表達出文章的主旨(有些報導是假的，有些是真的。)

Unit 3 Detail Questions

　　細節題在考題中佔的份量最大，細節題考的是：(1) 文章中提到的某人、某物、某個原因、理由、地點或時間等。(2) 你是否理解文章中某個詞語或某(幾) 個句子。

✳ 一般的出題形式

1. We can learn from the passage that _____ .

2. ...because _____ .

3. Which of the following is NOT a reason for...?

4. According to the passage, which of the following statements is true?

5. According to the passage, which of the following statements is NOT true?

6. The following are mentioned in this passage EXCEPT _____ ?

✳ 找尋細節的方法

1. 先從題目或選項中找到關鍵字。

2. 在文章中搜尋到這些關鍵字之後，仔細閱讀關鍵字前後的內容，找出答案。

Activities

以下有兩篇短文，請運用查讀技巧回答以下的細節題。

1.　　Esther Pauline Friedman Lederer, better known as Ann Landers, was the world's most widely read columnist. She had around 90 million readers and appeared in more than 1,200 newspapers. As a daughter of Russian immigrants born in 1918 in Sioux City, Iowa, she began writing her advice column on October 16, 1955 for the Chicago Sun-Times. Under Lederer's pen, the column quickly became one of the most favorite newspaper columns in the world, shadowed only perhaps by her twin sister's Dear Abby efforts. In fact, the two sisters, born only 17 minutes apart, competed against each other through their entire lives and finally reconciled in the mid-60's.

◼ _____(1) Ann Landers _____.

(A) had no brothers and sisters

(B) was born in Russia in 1918

(C) began to work as a columnist in 1955

◼ _____(2) Ann Landers' first advice column appeared in the _____.

(A) Chicago Tribune

(B) Chicago Sun-Times

(C) Chicago Daily News

◼ _____(3) Which of the following statements is NOT true?

(A) Ann Landers' parents emigrated from Russia to the U.S.

(B) Abby and Ann Landers started to compete in the mid-60's.

(C) Dear Abby is a famous advice column.

2.   Attempts are being made to record and preserve the languages which are in danger. That is done by compiling dictionaries and recording audio conversations and folk stories. For those languages that still have a reasonable number of speakers, local communities and even some national governments are encouraging the younger generation to learn and use their native tongue. Some successes have occurred with Scots in Britain, Gaelic in Ireland, Yupik in Alaska, and some Native American languages in the U.S.

◼ _____(1) Which of the following is NOT mentioned as a way of preserving endangered languages?

(A) Recording folk songs.

(B) Compiling dictionaries.

(C) Encouraging the younger generation to learn them.

■ _____ (2) Which language once faced or is facing extinction in Ireland?

(A) Scots.

(B) Gaelic.

(C) Yupik.

3.   During World War II, an American scientist, Percy Spencer, was developing a machine called a magnetron. It produced radio waves for radar systems to detect German warplanes. One day, after experimenting with the device, Spencer found that a chocolate bar in his pocket had completely melted. Then wisely standing farther away, Spencer placed some raw popcorn in front of the machine. Soon the corn was popping everywhere. Spencer had just invented the microwave oven.

■ _____ Which of the following is NOT true?

(A) The microwave oven was invented by Percy Spencer.

(B) The microwave oven was a by-product of another technology.

(C) Percy Spencer worked for a German company.

4.   An elephant's beautiful tusks are actually special teeth. They are used as weapons for sparring with other elephants and for defending against predators. Tusks are also tools for stripping bark from trees, gathering food, and digging for water.

■ _____ Which of the following is NOT stated in this passage?

(A) Elephants use their tusks to lift things.

(B) Elephants use their tusks to dig in the ground for water.

(C) Elephants use their tusks as weapons.

5. On May 18, 1980, Mount St. Helens in southwest Washington State erupted. At first people thought it was a forest fire, and then they knew it was a volcanic eruption.

The eruption of Mount St. Helens stunned scientists. At 8:32 a.m., an earthquake measuring 5.1 on the Richter scale occurred. That earthquake sparked a massive eruption, which lasted for nine hours. Within minutes a mushroom-shaped column of ash was seen come out, and then a massive explosion shot from the mountain top. The ash drifted and fell as far as 930 miles away. By the time the ash settled, 57 people were killed, many of whom disappeared beneath tons of ash. Hundreds of square miles of rich forests were changed into a grey, lifeless landscape. The total damage was estimated at more than one billion U.S. dollars.

In 1982, the Congress designated 110,000 acres surrounding the volcano as Mount St. Helens National Volcanic Monument for recreation and education.

■ _____ (1) According to the passage, which of the following is NOT true?

(A) The eruption began with an earthquake measuring 5.1 on the Richter scale.

(B) Losses caused by the eruption totaled more than $1 billion.

(C) The ash coming out of the volcano looked like a rocket.

■ _____ (2) The eruption of Mt. St. Helens lasted for about _____ .

(A) 7 hours.

(B) 8 hours.

(C) 9 hours.

■ _____ (3) The eruption turned hundreds of square miles of forests into _____ .

(A) a picturesque landscape

(B) a lifeless wasteland

(C) an area of wet land

_____(4) Mount St. Helens National Volcanic Monument _____.

    (A) was established in 1980

    (B) consists of 110,000 acres around the volcano

    (C) serves as a resource only for researchers

6.   A four-hour drive from London through beautiful countryside would bring you to Nottingham, which belongs to Robin in every sense. A smiling Robin pops up from every billboard, welcoming you in his territory. You may wonder why he's smiling so much. The smile keeps the cash counter ringing and the economy happy —more than 5 million tourists visit Nottingham every year.

Sherwood Forest is about half an hour's journey from there. In it, the giant oak tree, Robin Hood's hiding place, is the center of tourists' attention. The tree is huge; the statistics are awesome: weight 23 tons, width 33 feet, branch spread over 92 feet and age over a thousand years. It feels great to stand before a living witness of history.

_____(1) Which of the following is NOT true about the tree?

    (A) It is a huge oak tree.

    (B) It is in the Sherwood Forest.

    (C) It is five hundred years old.

_____(2) Who or what attracts 5 million tourists to Nottingham?

    (A) Robin Hood.

    (B) The countryside.

    (C) The drive from London.

Answer & Tip

1. ⑴ C　⑵ B　⑶ B　　2. ⑴ A　⑵ B　　3. C　　4. A

5. ⑴ C　⑵ C　⑶ B　⑷ B　　6. ⑴ C　⑵ A

解析

1. ⑴ 找到選項中的關鍵字(sister、1918、1955)後逐一搜尋答案。

　　⑵ 根據題目中的關鍵字(advice column)搜尋到答案就在同一句。

　　⑶ 選項中找到關鍵字(parents、compete、Dear Abby)後逐一搜尋哪一項是錯誤的。

2. ⑴ 題目中找到關鍵字(preserving)，文章中搜尋到第一句有 preserve，答案就在下一句。

　　⑵ 根據題目中的關鍵字 (Ireland) 搜尋，便可找到答案。

3. 這題和第一題技巧相同，但在段落中找不到 B 選項的關鍵字，就先看 A、C 選項是否找得到答案，如果找不到再讀其他部份看看是否有提到 B 選項所說的內容，微波爐是其他科技產物的副產品。

4. 選項中找到關鍵字 (lift things, dig, weapon) 後逐一搜尋段落中是否有敘述。用來防衛 (defend)，就是當武器 (as weapons)。

5. ⑴ 選項中找到關鍵字 (5.1, billion, ash) 後逐一去搜尋答案。

　　⑵ 根據選項中的關鍵字 (hours) 找答案。

　　⑶ 根據題目中的關鍵字 (forests) 搜尋。

　　⑷ 題目就是關鍵字，答案就在段落中最後一句。

6. ⑴ 根據題目中的關鍵字 (tree) 找到第二段的內容都在描述這棵樹。

　　⑵ 根據題目中的關鍵字 (tourists) 找到第一段最後一句。

字義題就是要讀者從文章中找到字義。

✳ 一般的出題形式

1. The word "×" in the...line/paragraph most likely means _____.

2. The word "×" in the...line/paragraph can be best replaced by _____.

3. The underlined word "×" in the...paragraph is closest in meaning to _____.

✳ 找尋細節的方法

可以利用關鍵字的上下文線索(Context Clues)來推測字義，這是很常用的閱讀技巧。這些線索包括：

1. 標點符號

   在「—(破折號)」、「:(冒號)」、「,(逗點)」之後或在「()(括弧)」之中會找到字詞的定義或解釋。

   Example (粗體字的字義可以由劃底線的部分推測出來)

   Polygraphers, the people who operate lie detectors, claim that they can establish guilt by detecting physiological changes that accompany emotional stress.

2. 慣用語或片語

   可以在 that is (那就是說)或 in other words (換句話說) 等之後找到重述的文字。另外在 for example 或 such as 之後可以找到相關的舉例說明。

   Example (粗體字的字義可以由劃底線的部分推測出來)

   A. Groups of musicians played together with **instruments** such as trumpets, saxophones, pianos and drums.

   B. The deceased person is **cremated**; that is, the body is burned and reduced to ashes.

3. 前後文

可以從字詞的同一句中(例如 and 前後有可能是同義詞，而 or 前後有可能是同義或反義詞)；也可從前後幾句或幾行的文意中(或許是描述、定義、同義詞或反義詞)瞭解字義。

Example (粗體字的字義可以由劃底線的部分推測出來)

A. This is a similar activity to **scanning** or search-reading, which is reading with a particular purpose in mind such as finding a specific word or phrase.

B. A U.S. Navy team **blasted** the fuel tanks of the Japanese freighter. It was set on fire deliberately.

C. British scientists said that they had developed an injection of a natural digestive hormone to help **obese** and overweight people lose weight.

Activities

I. 請將以下每一題中可以推測出粗體字詞意思的線索找出來，並且劃上底線。

1. **Virtual reality** is a new type of computer technology. It lets a user enter an artificial world that is completely different from reality.

2. No matter how much knowledge you have **accumulated** or gathered, you'll never make sound judgments if you don't have wisdom.

3. If you have never baked a cake before, it may take you months to make a beautiful cake that can stand upright without **collapsing**.

4. This brings us to two important words—"**hyperstress**" or too much stress and "**hypostress**" or not enough stress.

5. The most important step in Egyptian mummification is **dehydration**—the removal of all moisture from the body.

6. By **exhaling** air from the lungs in short bursts of laughter, breathing is quickened and heartbeats are increased, which achieve as much good as a ten-minute bike ride.

7. The ancient Egyptians used a sophisticated process to preserve the bodies of the dead, particularly their royalty, because they believed in **resurrection**—that the body as well as the spirit would rise again in the afterlife.

8. Exercise helps us lose weight by **curbing** hunger. When we exercise, body fat is released into bloodstream and our blood sugar doesn't drop. Low blood sugar is the most important factor that stimulates us to feel hungry. So when we exercise, we are likely to feel less hungry.

9. Most of us live terribly **sedentary** lives; when we're not sitting at our office desks, we're sitting on a bus or a train or in a car or in front of TV sets. We seldom go for a walk, let alone exercising very vigorously.

10. **Anaerobic** exercise refers to fitness routines that don't rely on oxygen for fuel. It typically involves short bursts of energy, which are powered by non-oxygen fuel sources.

II. 下面這篇文章有七個粗體字，請利用上下文的線索瞭解其字義後，完成文章之後的配合題。

    Bird **migration** is one of the world's most extraordinary wonders. Millions of birds travel thousands of miles, only to make their return journey a few months later. It is believed that they migrate to improve their chances of survival, usually because warmer climate provides a better environment for feeding, or especially for **rearing** their young.

    Birds become increasingly **restless** as the time for migration approaches. Some birds gather in flocks and practice short flights together before the final **departure**.

There are usually a lot of activities, noise and a sense of excitement and expectation.

The bird's brain can register how long the day is, and whether the length of the day is increasing or **decreasing**. The changing length of the day is probably the factor that **triggers** migratory behavior. In an experiment, scientists found that shorter periods of daylight change the hormone balance of birds, so that they **retain** more fat. This stored fat is the fuel that provides the energy for a long flight. It was also found that in longer periods of darkness, the glands of the birds become active and birds become more excited. No wonder most flocks of birds begin their migratory flight during the night.

_____ 1. migration   A. leaving

_____ 2. rear   B. to continue to have

_____ 3. restless   C. to become less, fewer, or shorter

_____ 4. departure   D. movement of birds from one place to another far away

_____ 5. decrease   E. to cause something to start

_____ 6. trigger   F. to look after or care for

_____ 7. retain   G. always moving about

III. 閱讀短文，並回答下面四題字義題。

Polar bears are referred to as the most **nomadic** of all bear species because they prefer to travel from one site to another where food is seasonally plentiful. Strictly speaking, they are **carnivores**. They eat meat, and seals are their primary prey. Sometimes they catch some species of whales and walruses.

Unlike brown and black bears, all polar bears do not **hibernate** in winter. They stay active all year round. However, pregnant polar bears dig dens and hibernate in the traditional sense. In late fall or early winter, they usually give birth to twin **cubs**. When born, cubs are usually 10 inches high and weigh 1.5 pounds.

_____(1) The word "nomadic" is closest in meaning to _____ .

    (A) plentiful

    (B) wandering

    (C) energetic

_____(2) Carnivores are animals that _____ .

    (A) mainly eat meat

    (B) are fed mainly on seafood

    (C) are skillful in finding prey

_____(3) The word "hibernate" most likely means to _____ .

    (A) remain active all year round

    (B) be in the state of deep sleep in the winter

    (C) dig dens to keep warm

_____(4) The word "cubs" can be best replaced by _____ .

    (A) births

    (B) families

    (C) babies

Answer & Tip

I. 1. an artificial world that is completely different from reality

  2. gathered

  3. stand upright

  4. too much stress; not enough stress

  5. the removal of all moisture from the body

  6. air from the lungs

  7. that the body as well as the spirit would rise again in the afterlife

8. when we exercise, we are likely to feel less hungry

9. sitting

10. fitness routines that don't rely on oxygen for fuel

II. 1. D   2. F   3. G   4. A   5. C   6. E   7. B

III. 1. B   2. A   3. B   4. C

解析

II. 1. 線索：travel thousands of miles

2. 線索：feeding, their young

3. 線索：Some birds gather in flocks and practice short flights together.... 和 a lot of activities

4. 線索：the time for migration approaches

5. 線索：or 之前的反義字 increasing

6. 線索：這個字之後三句解釋此因素如何促成遷移的行為

7. 線索：stored

III. 1. 線索：travel from one site to another

2. 線索：eat meat

3. 線索：stay active all year round

4. 線索：give birth to 和 when born

Unit 5　Inference Questions

類推題的答案是無法在文章裡直接找得到的，以下為一般的出題形式：

1. Which of the following can be inferred from the passage?
2. It can be inferred from the passage that _____.
3. This passage was most likely written by someone who _____.
4. The passage is most likely taken from _____.
5. We can conclude from the passage that _____.

✳ 何謂類推

類推 (inference) 就是根據文章中的證據，也就是作者暗示性的文字或明白陳述的事實或細節所做的合理猜測(guess)、判斷(judgment)或結論(conclusion)。

✳ 如何類推

　　將文章中所讀到的證據和日常生活中的認知或經驗結合起來，運用推理能力 (reasoning skill)、甚至直覺或判斷力推敲出文章中沒有直接敘述的隱含意思。例如看到 "Jane kept yawning in the first class." 這個句子，可以猜測 "Jane probably didn't sleep well last night."

　　其實在日常生活中就經常在練習類推，例如：老師發考卷的時候，看到某同學驚訝又喜悅的表情，一定會合理地判斷他很可能考得比預期的好。平日閱讀時就需要要求自己訓練這種能力，方法就是：(1) 隨時提出問題，例如什麼人？什麼職業？為什麼說這些話？(2) 根據文章證據做出合理的預測，來回答自己提出的問題，如果看到有新的證據出現再做修正。

Activities

I. 以下每一題都有一個生活中常聽到或看到的句子，從三個選項中找出最可能從這個句子類推出的答案。

_____ 1. In the past, tea produced in Taiwan was mainly exported.

(A) Nowadays tea grown in Taiwan is sold locally.

(B) In the past, people in Taiwan worked very hard.

(C) Nowadays most tea plants in Taiwan are grown in high mountains.

_____ 2. Parents recognize that films are a chance to persuade their reluctant children to pick up a book and give it a try.

(A) If children are reluctant to read, even their parents cannot persuade them to.

(B) Films may motivate children to read the books on which the films are based.

(C) Good readers are unwilling to miss the chance to learn how films are made.

_____ 3. Women are always advised not to stay out late in this area.

(A) Women in this area are unable to stay alert to potentially dangerous situations.

(B) The number of attacks on women at night is high in this area.

(C) Women had better take control of their own safety.

_____ 4. Our government, local authorities and private companies are prepared to invest greatly in the development of the tourism industry.

(A) Not only the government but also private enterprises are responsible for the tourism industry.

(B) Tourism can bring a wider range of economic benefits for our country.

(C) Tourism is not a contribution to our country's economy.

II. 以下有兩段短文，根據類推的結果 (inference)，找出文章中出現的證據 (evidence)。

1. The eagle-eyed Cindy follows in the path of other breakthrough toys like Sony's barking Robot Aibo, which was the first to popularize voice command in the late 1990s. Cindy takes Aibo's innovations one step beyond: she not only follows instructions but also recognizes shapes, colors, and words. The effect is a doll that appears to be learning. （取自 93 年指定科目考題）

■ Inference A: Cindy is a robot.

Evidence A: _____

Inference B: Cindy has artificial intelligence.

Evidence B: _____

2.　　　For many years, I was convinced that my suffering was due to my size. I believed that when the weight disappeared, it would take old wounds, hurts, and rejections with it.

　　　Many weight-conscious people also mistakenly believe that changing our bodies will fix everything. Perhaps our worst mistake is believing that being thin equals being loved, being special, and being cherished. We fantasize about what it will be like when we reach the long-awaited goal. We work very hard to realize this dream. Then, at last, we find ourselves there.

　　　But we often gain back what we have lost. Even so, we continue to believe that next time it will be different. Next time, we will keep it off. Next time, being thin will finally fulfill its promise of everlasting happiness, self-worth, and, of course, love.

　　　It took me a long while to realize that there was something more for me to learn about beauty. Beauty standards vary with culture. In Samoa a woman is not considered attractive unless she weighs more than 200 pounds. More importantly, if it's happiness that we want, why not put our energy there rather than on the size of our body? Why not look inside? Many of us strive hard to change our body, but in vain. We have to find a way to live comfortably inside our body and make friends with and cherish ourselves. When we change our attitudes toward ourselves, the whole world changes. （取自 94 年學科能力測驗考題）

■ Inference A: The author has been troubled by his/her weight.

Evidence A: _____

Inference B: The author did not succeed in losing weight.

Evidence B: _____

Inference C: The author comes to realize that whether we are happy or not depends on how we look at ourselves.

Evidence C: _____

III. 仔細讀以下每一個段落，類推並回答問題。

1.　　Sometimes we feel that life has played a trick on us. We feel like that life has made a fool out of us. However, if we really examine ourselves, we could often find that it is not life that gets us into trouble.

■ What might it be that gets us into trouble?

_____

2.　　I went to college with children of migrant farm workers. Though they are citizens of this country, they are treated with so much disregard that it is hard to believe it happens in a rich nation that is constantly pointing the finger at other countries for human rights abuses.

■ What might the nation be? The United States, North Korea, or Mexico?

_____

3.　　Mike was playing with his children on the beach when he heard the teen scream. "You could see him trying to get away, to get to shore, but the animal was all around him," he said.

　　Bill said he watched in horror as the teen's brother struggled to keep the animal off. It was so much like the movie *Jaws* with the pool of blood.

■ A. What animal attacked the teen boy? And where? On the beach or in the water?

_____

■ B. Was the victim injured?

_____

4.　　Last night when I read the article, my tears streamed down my cheeks. I've been wondering how to deal with my 80-year-old mom, who is facing some lifestyle changes due to a heart problem. The article gives me incredible insight into how my mom might be feeling. Now I know how to preserve her dignity by saying the right words to show my concern. As a member of the sandwich generation, I'm constantly seeking good advice on how to deal with the people I dearly love.

■ A. What does the article that the author read probably discuss?

_____

■ B. Does the article deeply touch the author's heart?

_____

■ C. Does the author have her own children?

_____

Answer & Tip

I. 1. A   2. B   3. B   4. B

II. 1. Evidence A: like Sony's barking Robot Aibo

　　Evidence B: She not only follows instructions but also recognizes shapes, colors, and words.

　2. Evidence A: my suffering was due to my size

　　Evidence B: But we often gain back what we have lost.

　　Evidence C: When we change our attitudes toward ourselves, the whole world changes.

III. 1. our personality/our ways of thinking/our ways of doing things

　2. The United States.

　3. A. It might be a shark that attacked the boy in the water.   B. Yes, he was.

　4. A. It probably discusses emotions of the aged who have health problems.

　　B. Yes, it does.   C. Yes, she has.

解析

III. 1. 證據：ourselves

　2. 證據：a rich nation that is constantly pointing the finger at other countries for human rights abuses

　3. 證據：A. the movie *Jaws* 和 get to shore   B. the pool of blood

　4. 證據：A. 證據：80-year-old mom 和 insight into how my mom might be feeling

　　B. 證據：tears streamed down my cheeks

　　C. 證據：a member of the sandwich generation

Unit 6 Reference Questions

　　這類題目要測試你是否能正確指認出代名詞的指涉對象 (referents)。指涉對象可能是一個字、一個詞、一個子句或句子，能夠正確指認對瞭解文意大有幫助。以下為一般的出題形式：

1. The pronoun ◯ in line/paragraph 4 refers to _____.
2. The pronoun ◯ in the 3rd line/paragraph most likely refers to _____.

✳ 何謂代名詞的指涉對象

　　文章中經常會出現代名詞，包括 it、they、them、this、these、that、one，甚至是關係代名詞 which 或 that 等，而代名詞的指涉對象就是代名詞所指的字、詞，或者是一個子句或句子。

✳ 如何找尋代名詞的指涉對象

　　因為文章中必須先出現名詞與子句，之後才會有代名詞，所以指涉詞就要往前尋找。找到有可能性的指涉對象之後，再閱讀前後文意確認。例如：

Hikers then post the coordinates at www.geocaching.com, where other hikers can use **them**, along with a global positioning system (GPS), to join the worldwide goose chase.

→ them 之前可以找到 hikers 和 coordinates 兩個複數名詞，把這兩個名詞分別放在 them 的位置，就可以看出哪個符合邏輯。

Activities

I. 以下每一題都有一個以粗體標示的代名詞，請找出它的指涉對象，劃上底線。

1. Charles recalled how poor his family was in his 1978 autobiography, "Brother Ray:" "Even compared to other blacks...**we** were on the bottom of the ladder looking up at everyone else. Nothing was below us except the ground."

2. The soybean has a long history in agriculture. **It** has been cultivated for about 5,000 years. The first written record of soybean farming appeared when the Chinese emperor, Shen Nong, wrote about soybeans' medicinal properties.

3. It was not until the late 1500s that the kite appeared in Europe. In the 1700s, kites began to be used for scientific research. To learn more about the wind and the weather, recently scientists attached special instruments and cameras to kites and then flew **them** high into the sky. The creators of early flying machines, such as the airplane, used the kite as a model as well.

4. Modern hunters are equipped with powerful weapons, but for most of them, hunting is more for pleasure than for food. Because many big animals like lions, tigers and elephants are decreasing in number rapidly, **they** can no longer be hunted at will.

5. Some dieters find it helpful to drink a glass of water when they feel hungry between meals or just before meals. However, doctors do not recommend **this** as a regular way to achieve appetite reduction.

6. A great step forward was the use of movable type. The Chinese discovered **this** in the 11th century, but it was not known in Europe until 1440.

7. One of the first European books to be printed in movable type was Johannes Gutenberg's 42-line bible. The first book to be printed likewise in English was about the history of Troy. **It** was printed in Flanders in 1474 by an Englishman, William Caxton.

8. The dog and the blind handler also undergo training to work together. In this joint training, the handler learns how to command and understand the dog's movements, while the dog learns to move at the handler's pace and obey **him**.

9. While traveling, we often feel safer with a group of friends. In fact, a crowd of tourists talking or laughing loudly, and not paying much attention to what is going

on around **them**, can draw unwanted attention from thieves.

10. Man's best friend could also be a lifesaver in the fight against cancer. Scientists indicate that dogs have a sense of smell that is greater than **that** of humans. So they can be used to detect bladder cancer by smelling urine.

11. During the 2003-2004 school year, almost 80% of American schools offered free breakfast. The Government spent US$ 1.8 billion providing these meals. Some schools even offered free breakfast to all students. Now **they** have realized that it can be embarrassing for children from poor families to eat breakfast at school in front of their wealthier classmates.

II. 請回答每段短文之後有關字義的問題。

1. White fur allows polar bears to blend in with their snowy surroundings in the far north. This is useful since **it** disguises **them** from hunters. It also provides camouflage when the bears find themselves being hunted. Besides, the fur's main job is to act as the first line of defense against the weather.

　■＿＿＿＿(1) The pronoun "it" in the 2nd line refers to ＿＿.

　　　　　(A) north　(B) white fur　(C) prey

　■＿＿＿＿(2) The pronoun "them" in the 2nd line refers to ＿＿.

　　　　　(A) polar bears　(B) surroundings　(C) the weather

2. Underneath all that white fur, a polar bear's skin is actually black. This makes sense because black readily absorbs light. Black skin can absorb the warmth from the sunlight and hold **it** in, instead of reflecting it away.

　■＿＿＿＿The pronoun "it" in the 3rd line refers to ＿＿.

　　　　　(A) black skin　(B) warmth　(C) sunlight

3. Three long-finned pilot whales were rescued from a mass stranding on Cape Cod. The three whales were taken in a van to an aquarium, where they were kept in

a 60,000-gallon tank for several months. Only a few people worked with the whales so that **they** would not become too accustomed to human beings. Four months later they were released at sea.

■ _____ The pronoun "they" in the 4th line refers to _____ .

(A) people   (B) whales   (C) pilots

4.   In the winter, smaller mammals lose heat more quickly than larger **ones**. **They** must burn up their fat fast to keep warm. This is why mice make themselves underground during the winter, and sleep there on the coldest days. In this way, **they** save energy by being inactive. Squirrels also save energy by sleeping through spells of bad weather. Foxes and deer can remain active throughout the winter because of their larger size.

■ _____ (1) The pronoun "ones" in the 1st line refers to _____ .

(A) days   (B) mammals   (C) mice

■ _____ (2) The pronoun "they" in the 1st line refers to _____ .

(A) larger ones   (B) mice   (C) smaller mammals

■ _____ (3) The pronoun "they" in the 4th line refers to _____ .

(A) squirrels   (B) mice   (C) foxes

5.   In the early years, the Nelis family grew vegetables to sell locally or at the Chicago produce markets. During the Great Depression, a cousin in the Netherlands advised the family to plant daffodils. **They** took the advice and grew daffodils. Several years later they added crops of tulips. **This** dramatically changed life for the Nelis family. By the late 1930s, the family's tulip farm had become a "hot spot" for tourists flocking to Holland, Michigan.

■ _____ (1) The pronoun "They" in the 3rd line refers to _____ .

(A) the Netherlands   (B) the Nelis family   (C) daffodils

■ _____(2) The pronoun "This" in the 4th line refers to _____ .

    (A) Several years later they added crops of tulips.

    (B) A cousin in the Netherlands advised the family to plant daffodils.

    (C) The family's tulip farm had become a "hot spot."

6.   The Black Death started in West Asia in the 1330s. In 1347, Italian sailors brought the disease home with **them**. As people were quickly catching **it** and dying, the wealthy tried to escape by moving north. **They** did not know that they were bringing the disease with them and infecting new population. By 1350, the disease had reached as far north as Norway and Sweden.

■ _____(1) The pronoun "them" in the 2rd line refers to _____ .

    (A) routes   (B) sailors   (C) the wealthy

■ _____(2) The pronoun "it" in the 2th line refers to _____ .

    (A) the disease   (B) the matter   (C) China

■ _____(3) The pronoun "They" in the 3th line refers to _____ .

    (A) routes   (B) sailors   (C) the wealthy

Answer & Tip

I. 1. his poor family

2. soybean

3. kites

4. big animals

5. to drink a glass of water when they feel hungry between meals or just before meals

6. movable type

7. the first book to be printed likewise in English about the history of Troy

8. the handler

9. a crowd of tourists

10. a sense of smell

11. Some schools

II. 1.(1) B (2) A   2. B   3. B

　　4.(1) B (2) C (3) B   5.(1) B (2) A

　　6.(1) B (2) A (3) C

解析

解題方式請參考本章第一頁的解說。

Unit 7 Purpose or Tone Questions

日常生活中，收到一封 e-mail、一份傳真或一則信息時，其內容通常都有一定的目的。 文章也是如此， 但作者有時候不會在文章中直接明白地敘述其目的(Purpose)，因此目的題的答案就比較不容易在文章裡直接找到。而調性 (tone) 通常是指作者寫文章的語調、心情或態度。以下為一般的出題形式：

1. This passage is written mainly to _____.
2. The purpose of this passage is to _____.
3. What is the writer's main purpose of writing this passage?
4. What is the author's attitude toward...?
5. Which of the following best describes the tone of this passage?

✳ 何謂目的或調性

文章的目的可能是：

to inform	to criticize/praise	to amuse/entertain	to warn...about...
to explain	to give an opinion	to describe the history of...	
to persuade	to compare...and....	to propose solutions to...	
to describe/discuss problems		to encourage/urge readers to...	

文章的調性或作者的態度可能是：

indifferent	neutral	ironic	positive	negative	sarcastic
sympathetic	cheerful	hopeful	angry	depressed	humorous

✳ 如何尋找目的和調性 / 態度的方法

文章的目的和調性 / 態度都是需要細心體會的，通常目的可以由主題句、主旨及支持細節來判斷。另外，不同性質的文章語調自然是不同的，如果作者只是提供事實、陳述資料，其調性就是 informational。如果作者很輕鬆地談一些有趣的事，其調性就會是 humorous。至於作者對某事的態度是正面／贊成、負面／反對、或是很中立，只要仔細閱讀就不難由文意中判斷。

Activities

以下有八篇短文，細讀並判斷其調性或目的。

1.　　Laughter can help increase our ability to fight disease. It relaxes the body and reduces problems like high blood pressure and strokes. Some research suggests that laughter may also reduce the risk of heart disease. Historically, research has shown that distressing emotions are related to heart disease. A study done at the Maryland Medical Center suggests that laughter as well as a good sense of humor can protect us from heart disease. So try to laugh more. A laugh a day keeps the doctor away.

　■　_____This passage was written mainly to _____.

　　(A) explain how stress is related to heart disease

　　(B) persuade people to laugh more to stay healthy

　　(C) describe the research on heart disease

2.　　As a vegetarian, I am amazed at the outcry about eating dogs from people who quite happily eat fish, cows, pigs, goats and birds. What is the difference between eating dogs and pigs anyway? Is it because the former are more intelligent?

　■　_____Which of the following best describes the tone of this passage?

　　(A) Cheerful.　　(B) Sympathetic.　　(C) Sarcastic.

3.　　The uniform of a graduating student dates back to the medieval era. At the time, education was provided by the Church; therefore, many universities adopted robes similar to those worn by monks or priests. This tradition continues until today, with graduating students wearing gowns similar to medieval robes. The cap worn along with the gown also originated in the clothing of monks, who wore such headgear to protect their shaven heads from cold or injury.

■ _____ The passage is to _____.

(A) describe the tradition of priests' robes

(B) explain why graduating students wear gowns and caps

(C) introduce the origin of the uniform of medieval monks

4.　　Some language experts claim that learning a second language at a young age hinders progress in a child's mother tongue. They also argue that young children attending schools where English is spoken full time have less time for other subjects and might not perform so well in these subjects. However, they ignore the fact that studying another language can stimulate children's brains, and this may have a positive bearing on their other studies. Children under the age of six have a "sensitive" period, after which learning becomes more difficult. Far from retarding native language skills, learning a second language at a young age actually yields benefits.

■ _____ What's the author's attitude towards kids learning a second language at a young age?

(A) Positive.　(B) Negative.　(C) Indifferent.

5.　　Fallingwater has been considered to be one of the greatest examples of modern architecture. It's true that you can find quite a few innovative and clever things, but unfortunately, as a whole, it is a work of art rather than a house to live in. Wright made the house organic by building it out of the stone of the waterfall. As a result, the rough floor of cut stone is uneven. This makes it difficult for chairs to balance in some areas of the rooms. What's worse, the house leaks. Water seeps through the rock wall. The simple drain placed in the floor makes people there feel uncomfortable. The house is grand, but it fails as a good one.

■ _____ What is the main purpose of this passage?

(A) To compare.　(B) To praise.　(C) To criticize.

6.　　A pilot has more responsibilities than an average 9-to-5 workers do. First and foremost, a pilot is responsible for the lives of his passengers and crew. Every person who steps onto a plane puts trust in the pilot to take off and touch down safely and timely, no matter what circumstances come up. Bad weather, system failures, and security breaches are just a few of the major concerns that pilots have to come up against. Most pilots also have critical non-flying duties, such as balancing luggage and keeping logbooks. Besides their responsibilities for the passengers, they are also in charge of a 50 or 60 million dollar airplane that does not belong to them!

■ _____ The passage is written mainly to _____ .

(A) describe the career as a professional pilot

(B) discuss the responsibilities a pilot bears

(C) explain the strict requirements pilots should meet

7.　　After a long day working in the office, Alexander hailed a taxi to take him home. After informing the driver of his destination, Alexander restored to his reading of Dan Brown's intelligent thriller, *the Da Vinci Code*. About five minutes later, he suddenly looked up and noticed that the driver had detoured from the familiar route. To redirect the driver, Alexander tapped him on the shoulder. Out of the blue, the driver screamed, lost control of the car, and almost hit a bus. The cab went up on the footpath and finally stopped centimeters away from a shop window. For a second, everything went quiet in the cab. Then the driver said, "Look, mate! Don't ever do that again. You scared the living daylights out of me!" Alexander apologized and said, "I didn't realize that a little tap would scare you so much." The driver replied, "Sorry, sir. It's not really your fault. Today is my first day as a cab driver. I've been driving a funeral van for the last 2 years."

（取自 94 年指定科目考題）

■ _____ The main purpose of this passage is to _____.

(A) inform　(B) criticize　(C) entertain

8.　　The Royal Yacht Britannia is one of the world's most famous ships. Launched at John Brown's Shipyard in Clydebank in 1953, the Royal Yacht proudly served Queen and the UK for forty-four years. During that time Britannia carried the Queen and the Royal Family on 968 official voyages, from the South Seas to Antarctica.

　　At the beginning of January 1997, Britannia set sail from Portsmouth to Hong Kong on her last and longest voyage. On 11th December, 1997, Britannia was decommissioned at Portsmouth Naval Base in the presence of the Queen, the Duke of Edinburgh and fourteen senior members of the Royal Family.

　　Four months later, after intense competition from cities around the UK, the Government announced that Edinburgh was successful in its bid to become Britannia's new home. She is now owned by The Royal Yacht Britannia Trust, a charitable organization whose sole duty is the maintenance of Britannia in keeping her former role. Britannia is now permanently in Edinburgh's historic port of Leith and visitors can step on board the ship that was once home to the world's most famous family.

(From: http://www.royalyachtbritannia.co.uk.

Reproduced by permission of the Royal Yacht Britannia Trust.)

■ _____ This article was written mainly to _____ .

(A) describe the history of Britannia

(B) explain why the Britannia is world-wide famous

(C) discuss how the Britannia served the Queen and the Royal Family

Answer & Tip

1. B   2. C   3. B   4. A   5. C   6. B   7. C   8. A

解析

1. 由最後兩句得知其目的是鼓勵人笑，每天笑可以不用去看醫生。

2. 最後兩個問句：吃豬和吃狗有何不同?狗比較聰明嗎?諷刺葷食者反對吃狗肉。

3. 這一段說明畢業服的由來。選項 (C) 指僧侶服的由來。

4. 一、二句提出反方說法，第三句之後辯駁，結論句明白指出贊成的立場。

5. 從第二句 but 之後作者都在批評此建築。

6. 主題句就指出段落主旨：飛行員的責任比朝九晚五的上班族重。

7. 這個有趣的小故事目的當然是讓娛樂讀者。

8. 本篇介紹 Britannia 這艘船從替皇室服務至目前的歷史。

Note

測驗篇

The Curse of the Iceman

A German tourist named Helmut Simon was hiking in the Austrian mountains at the end of the summer in 1991. Suddenly, he saw the preserved, frozen body of a leather-clothed man lying on the icy ground. Simon reported his discovery, believing he had found a hunter who died in the cold weather a few hundred years earlier. A professional mountaineer, Kurt Fritz, then led a team of scientists headed by Dr. Rainer Henn to the site. A few weeks later, the mummy's transfer to a science lab was broadcast around the world in a documentary film.

Then, one by one, people who had been in contact with the prehistoric mummy began to die. First, Dr. Rainer Henn was killed in a car crash on his way to give a lecture about the mummy in 1992. Next, the mountaineer Kurt Fritz was killed by a huge pile of falling snow while hiking. After the two accidents, there was talk in the media that the "Iceman" had brought bad luck. When Rainer Hoelzl also died of a mysterious illness a few months after his TV program about the mummy, the story spread that the Iceman might be cursed.

The discoverer, Helmut Simon, believed these tales to be ridiculous. After winning the right to earn money from "mummy tourists," he decided to celebrate by again hiking in the mountains. He died when he fell off a 200-meter cliff in a sudden snowstorm. Later, the new scientific team's leader, Konrad Spindler, died weeks after publicly saying the deaths were just unfortunate accidents. Finally, in 2005, Dr. Tom Loy died before he could finish a book on the Iceman.

_____ 1. What is the main idea of the passage?

(A) People generally believe that the Iceman's deadly curse is simply ridiculous.

(B) In spite of some scientists' efforts, many questions about the Iceman's life and death remain unsolved.

(C) Hundreds of scientists have been involved in the study of the well-preserved mummy.

(D) Rumor has it that people who came into contact with the Iceman died as the result of a curse.

_____ 2. According to the passage, how many people with connections to the Iceman were killed?

(A) Three.　(B) Four.　(C) Five.　(D) Six.

_____ 3. The Iceman was found _____.

(A) wearing leather clothes

(B) a few hundred years ago

(C) by a mountaineer, Kurt Fritz

(D) by a German archeologist

_____ 4. According to the passage, which of the following is true?

(A) The rumor about the curse began in 1992 with the death of Rainer Hoelzl.

(B) Rainer Henn, a filmmaker, died of a mysterious illness.

(C) Helmut Simon was killed during an unexpected snowstorm.

(D) Kurt Fritz, the head of the team, died in a car crash while on his way to give a talk about the Iceman.

_____ 5. Which of the following might be what Konrad Spindler said publicly weeks before he died?

(A) "The curse is entirely an invention of the media."

(B) "Rumors of the deadly curse will continue to swirl."

(C) "The mummy is cursed."

(D) "I'm afraid the curse is probably true."

Unit 02

All about Chocolate

The Mayans, who once ruled over parts of Mexico and South America, are believed to have first discovered chocolate as early as 500 AD. The cocoa plant is a native of that region, and chocolate is produced from the cocoa plant's seeds. The Mayans discovered that a drink made from the powdered seeds could increase their muscle size and **boost** their energy.

Hundreds of years later, when the Aztecs came into power, the popularity of chocolate grew even further. The Aztecs believed that chocolate had healing powers and reserved it only for kings, royals and warriors.

Europe remained unaware of chocolate's existence until the middle of the sixteenth century. Christopher Columbus, in one of his many voyages to the Americas, observed that the natives held the nut-shaped beans in great respect; he mistook them as small-sized almonds. However, it was only when another Spanish explorer, Hernando Cortez, traveled to the Americas a few years later and tried the drink that Europe came to know of its existence for the first time.

Although it was the Spanish who brought chocolate to Europe, countries like France, England and the Netherlands soon began to cultivate cocoa plants in their colonies. With an increase in supply, the prices lowered, and the masses could enjoy the delicious drink. People began to experiment, and soon chocolate appeared in cakes and pastries. It wasn't until 1828 that the true "chocolate invasion" of the world took place when Conrad J. van Houten, a Dutch chocolate maker, discovered an easier way to produce cocoa powder.

Building on Houten's technique, English chocolate maker Joseph Storrs Fry produced the first chocolate for eating in 1847 by re-mixing the cocoa powder with cocoa butter. Each cocoa bean contains about 54% cocoa butter, a natural fat. The milk chocolates that we cherish so much today were first invented by

Henri Nestle of Switzerland when he mixed powdered milk with the other ingredients.

_____ 1. The passage is mainly about _____ .
  (A) how cocoa powder was produced in an easier way
  (B) how chocolate was a profitable industry for Spain
  (C) a brief history of chocolate
  (D) the healing powers of chocolate

_____ 2. The word "boost" in the first paragraph can be best replaced by
  " _____ ."
  (A) endure   (B) increase   (C) decrease   (D) distinguish

_____ 3. Who first found an easier way to produce cocoa powder and introduced it to the world?
  (A) Conrad J. van Houten   (B) Joseph Storrs Fry
  (C) Henri Nestle   (D) Hernando Cortez

_____ 4. European people began to know about chocolate in _____ .
  (A) 1828   (B) the mid-16th century
  (C) 1849   (D) the year Columbus discovered America

_____ 5. According to the passage, which of the following is NOT true?
  (A) Chocolate was not accessible to all of the Aztecs.
  (B) The Mayans were the first to create a beverage from crushed cocoa beans.
  (C) European countries planted cocoa trees in their colonies; as a result, the supply increased and the prices decreased.
  (D) An English chocolate company invented a way of adding milk to chocolate, creating what is known as milk chocolates.

All Eyes on London

Architects David Marks and Julia Barfield made their first drawing of the London Eye in 1993. They entered a contest in England to build a millennium landmark as the 20th century came to an end. Unfortunately, no one won, and the project was completely cancelled. However, Marks and Barfield refused to give up and continued with their plans to realize their dream of creating "something uplifting" for the coming century. Their dream attracted the attention of the general public. With financial help from British Airways, the London Eye was finally completed and opened to the public in March 2000. All eyes have been on London ever since.

The London Eye——or the Millennium Wheel, as it is sometimes called—— looks like a giant bicycle wheel. Hanging from it are 32 passenger capsules. People board the capsules, which are pulled up to 135 meters above the ground. Because the wheel rotates very slowly, it does not have to stop for passengers to get on the capsules. It takes about 30 minutes for a capsule to complete a rotation. On any given day, the wheel can take 15,000 sightseers and can rotate about 22 times.

There are simple reasons why the London Eye is the city's premiere tourist destination. Since it stands in the heart of London, the wheel gives visitors an astonishing view of the city. From each of the capsules, visitors can see 25 miles in any direction. Thus, one can easily spot world-famous landmarks of London, such as Buckingham Palace, St. Paul's Cathedral and Westminster Abbey. Visitors can also rent one of the air-conditioned capsules for private parties. Each capsule can **accommodate** up to 25 people——enough for a cozy get-together with wine, food and fantastic views.

Other cities, like Las Vegas and Shanghai, are planning to outdo the Eye.

However, it will always be the first of its kind.

_____ **1.** The London Eye was mainly built to _____ .
   (A) mark the millennium
   (B) set a new record
   (C) provide a new recreation site
   (D) get the competition to heat up

_____ **2.** How long does it take for passengers to complete a rotation?
   (A) Fifteen minutes.   (B) Twenty-two minutes.
   (C) Twenty-five minutes.   (D) Thirty minutes.

_____ **3.** The word "accommodate" in the third paragraph can be replaced by
   "_____ ."
   (A) crowd   (B) entertain   (C) guard   (D) hold

_____ **4.** The wheel doesn't need to stop to take on passengers because _____ .
   (A) it is impossible to stop once it starts to rotate
   (B) it rotates so slowly that it's easy for passengers to get on
   (C) it can save a lot more energy this way
   (D) this can make passengers more excited

_____ **5.** According to the passage, which of the following is NOT true?
   (A) One of the reasons for the London Eye's popularity is that visitors can
       enjoy the great view from the heart of London.
   (B) When passengers ride on the London Eye, they can see landmarks as far
       as 25 miles.
   (C) Construction of the London Eye, designed by British Airway, began in
       1993.
   (D) The London Eye includes 32 air-conditioned passenger capsules.

Tour de Lance

Born in Texas in 1971, Lance Armstrong was a gifted athlete from his early teens on. He started out as a triathlete but turned his attention to amateur cycling soon after. He started racing and was on the American Olympic team in 1992 before turning professional. After finishing last in his first professional race, the *Clasicade de San Sebastian*, he determined that it would never happen again.

He went on to win races and made a name for himself. Unfortunately, when he got off his bike after a race in 1996, he felt a pain. It turned out to be testicular cancer, which had spread through most of his body when diagnosed. Doctors didn't give him much of a chance, but he underwent treatment for three years and dramatically survived.

He made his comeback in 1999 by winning his first *Tour de France*, which he did not lose for the next six years. He got more than just a **trophy**; he became a legend. Some people call the race the "Tour de Lance" to honor Lance Armstrong. He has since retired from racing, but he is not finished yet. In addition to his charity work to raise money for cancer awareness and research, he has also made appearances in movies.

He is not only a tough person but also a good role model for young people. In his book, *It's Not About the Bike*, he says that when he is a hundred years old, he wants to race down through the Alps and see people cheering him on to victory; only then would he go and lie down in the beautiful French fields to die in grace.

_____ 1. Lance Armstrong won the *Tour de France* _____.

    (A) six times in a row from 1999 to 2004

    (B) six times in a row from 1992 to 1997

    (C) seven times in a row from 1999 to 2005

    (D) seven times in a row from 1997 to 2002

_____ 2. When Lance Armstrong finished his first professional race, he was probably

    _____.

    (A) doubtful   (B) determined

    (C) desperate   (D) defeated

_____ 3. Which of the following is NOT true about Lance Armstrong's cancer?

    (A) He was diagnosed with testicular cancer in 1996.

    (B) It had spread to many areas of his body when he found out about it.

    (C) After three years' treatment, he recovered and returned to cycling.

    (D) Doctors told him his odds of survival were pretty high.

_____ 4. The word "trophy" in the 3rd paragraph is probably a(n) _____.

    (A) benefit   (B) prize   (C) defeat   (D) obstacle

_____ 5. Which of the following is NOT stated in this passage?

    (A) Armstrong started his sporting career as a triathlete.

    (B) Armstrong has raised funds to support cancer research and to raise
        people's awareness of cancer.

    (C) Armstrong founded the Lance Armstrong Foundation in 1997.

    (D) Armstrong wants to win another cycling victory at 100 and lie down in
        the French fields to die gracefully.

Unit 05

The Surgeons of the Future

D id you know that some surgeries today are carried out by robotic, rather than human, surgeons? These surgeons are machines developed to perform certain operations that can be difficult to do with human hands, because they require a lot of small, precise actions.

Most robotic surgeons, such as the "Da Vinci Surgical System," don't replace a doctor completely, but instead help the human surgeon to perform an operation more accurately. The "Da Vinci" is made up of a robot with four arms and a "viewing console," which is a TV screen with a control panel. Three of the robotic surgeons' arms hold surgical instruments, and the fourth contains a camera, which sends images to the viewing console. Through this, a human surgeon in a neighboring room watches the pictures on the TV screen, and guides the robot.

Not everyone agrees on the benefits of using robotic surgeons. Some people worry that robots are not able to realize when they are making a mistake, and feel that human minds are still more reliable than a machine. They are particularly worried by the prediction that robots in the future will perform operations without any human surgeon involved at all. Other people point to the high cost of these machines, as well as the extra time and money it takes to train staff to use them.

Nevertheless, robotic surgery is a fast-growing field. The most important advantage, say supporters, is that a robotic hand does not tremble like a human hand. Therefore, it can perform quicker and more accurate operations. This means that more operations can be carried out every day, with a higher rate of success. With new systems appearing on the market each year, it seems that robotic surgeons, despite their critics, are indeed the surgeons of the future.

_____ 1. The passage was written mainly to _____ .
    (A) introduce robotic surgeons
    (B) introduce the Da Vinci Surgical System
    (C) discuss the advantages of robotic surgery
    (D) discuss the disadvantages of robotic surgery

_____ 2. Which of the following is NOT true about the Da Vinci Surgical System?
    (A) It is made up of a robot and a viewing console.
    (B) The images seen from the viewing console are sent by a camera attached to one of the arms.
    (C) It can completely replace human surgeons.
    (D) The viewing console is set up in a room next to the operating room.

_____ 3. According to the passage, which of the following is the main reason for using surgical robots?
    (A) Longer surgery time.   (B) Less recovery time.
    (C) Convenience.   (D) Precision.

_____ 4. Which of the following is NOT mentioned as one of some people's worries about robotic surgery?
    (A) Surgical robots cost too much.
    (B) Robotic surgery takes longer than traditional surgery.
    (C) In the future, surgical robots will completely replace human surgeons.
    (D) It takes additional time and money for doctors and nurses to learn to use the robots.

_____ 5. What is the author's attitude toward robotic surgeon?
    (A) For it.   (B) Against it.
    (C) Neutral.   (D) Compromise.

The Popularity of Sudoku

Sudoku, also known as "Number Place," was originally designed by Howard Garns, an American architect and puzzle maker. In the late 1970s, the puzzle was first published in New York by *Dell Magazines*. In 1984, a Japanese puzzle company introduced it to Japanese fans. The puzzle soon took Japan by storm and was later named Sudoku, which means "single number" in Japanese.

In 1997, Wayne Gould, a retired Hong Kong judge, came across a Sudoku puzzle in a Tokyo bookshop. He spent six years developing a computer program that could create the puzzles quickly. He then sold his software to *The Times*. On November 12, 2004, a Sudoku puzzle first appeared in the newspaper in London, and it has been printed daily ever since. After a few months, many other British newspapers started publishing their own Sudoku puzzles. In April 2005, the puzzle came back to New York. The Sudoku craze quickly spread all over the U.S.

Today, Sudoku has indeed become a global phenomenon. There are Sudoku clubs, books, and websites. Sudoku can now be played on a mobile phone or a computer, as well as with just a pen and paper. There is even a Sudoku competition! The first world Sudoku championship was held in Italy on March 10 to 12, 2006. Eighty-five people took part, and the event was won by Jana Tylova, an accountant from the Czech Republic. She said, "I like Sudoku because all you need is a piece of paper, a pencil, and some logical thinking and patience."

Nobody can deny the fact that people of all ages enjoy the popular puzzle, which provides mentally engaging activity. In some schools, sudoku puzzles are adopted as exercises for their students to stimulate their thinking. Some experts even suggest that older people solve Sudoku puzzles to prevent the development of Alzheimer's disease and memory loss.

_____ **1.** According to the passage, solving Sudoku puzzles requires _____ .
  (A) logic and patience (B) new computer equipment
  (C) advanced mathematical abilities (D) rapid calculation

_____ **2.** How many years had passed before Sudoku came back to the U.S. and became popular?
  (A) About 11 years. (B) About 15 years
  (C) About 30 years. (D) About 50 years

_____ **3.** Sudoku originated in _____ .
  (A) the U.S. (B) Japan (C) Britain (D) Italy

_____ **4.** According to the passage, which of the following is NOT true?
  (A) In 2006, for the first time, Sudoku lovers from all over the world had a chance to challenge one another in Italy.
  (B) Today, the Sudoku craze has spread around the world.
  (C) Sudoku quickly became a huge hit after it was introduced in Japan.
  (D) It took Wayne Gould eight years to develop a computer program to create puzzles quickly.

_____ **5.** Doctors suggest that older people play Sudoku because it _____ .
  (A) enhances their reading ability
  (B) stimulates thinking
  (C) makes them more patient than young people
  (D) is very easy to solve

Marked for Life?

The term *tattoo* originated from the Tahitian word *tatau*, which means "to mark." Tattoos date back to prehistoric times, when people were tattooed to identify tribes or families, mark criminals, keep away various illness, and idolize gods. In the late 1700s, Captain Cook returned from the South Pacific to London, bringing back a heavily tattooed Polynesian named Omai. He caused a **sensation**, and tattooing soon became a craze among England's upper class.

In the U.S., during the Civil War, soldiers got tattooed in memory of their dead comrades and their military career. However, it was not until the invention of the electric tattooing machine in 1891 by Samuel O'Reilly in New York that tattooing became available to almost anyone. The upper class turned away from it as a result of its popularity. Many criminals used tattoos to record their crimes and prison sentences. This cultural use of tattoos caused many people to associate **them** with crimes.

In the mid-1900s, tattooing still had a very bad image. With cases of hepatitis infection reported in newspapers, tattooing was even considered dangerous and declined in popularity. In the late 1960s, however, attitudes towards tattooing changed considerably, as many famous people began to get them. Lyle Tuttle, an American who knew how to use the media, brought the underground art form of tattooing into the mainstream. Today, an increasing number of people are following this trend.

People have to take many things into consideration before getting a tattoo. It is quite painful if people later want to remove their tattoos, and it can cost much more than the tattoo itself. What's more, tattoos may spread blood-born diseases such as AIDS and hepatitis B and C.

_____ **1.** In prehistoric times, people were tattooed for several reasons, EXCEPT

_____ .

(A) health   (B) art

(C) religion   (D) culture

_____ **2.** The word "sensation" in the first paragraph can be best replaced by

" _____ ."

(A) panic   (B) barrier

(C) stir   (D) defense

_____ **3.** The pronoun "them" in the 2nd paragraph refers to _____ .

(A) tattoos   (B) many people

(C) crimes   (D) prison sentences

_____ **4.** According to the passage, which of the following is NOT true?

(A) Today, tattooing is on the rise in popularity.

(B) Omai was introduced to London by Captain Cook.

(C) In the mid-1900s, tattooing was unpopular because of hepatitis infections.

(D) Lyle Tuttle invented the first electric tattooing machine.

_____ **5.** It can be inferred from the passage that _____ .

(A) during World War II, soldiers in Europe were crazy about tattooing

(B) no royal family members in Europe got themselves tattooed

(C) in the early 1900s, tattoo artists gained respect from the general public

(D) before electric tattooing machines were invented, tattooing was popular among the upper class

Snowboarding

Many people think of snowboarding as a relatively modern sport, invented and made popular by teens looking for a way to ride their skateboards during the winter. However, the history of snowboarding actually dates back to 1929 when the first snowboard-like device was made.

That first "snowboard" was invented by a man named Jack Burchett, who attempted to secure a sheet of plywood to his feet with clothesline so that he could ski downhill. This was the basic model for over 30 years until the next major step in the sport took place. In 1965, the "Snurfer" was invented by Sherman Poppen as a toy for his daughter. He bound two skis together and attached a rope to the front end for steering. He soon put his idea into production, and one million Snurfers were sold over the next ten years.

Since then, the snowboard has undergone many changes, such as the attachment of bindings, which are used to hold a rider to the board. Boards are also shaped differently. Though it's been almost 80 years since the concept of the snowboard was introduced, it's only in the last fifteen years that the sport has really become popular with winter sports enthusiasts.

Snowboarding made its first major international appearance at the 1998 Winter Olympics. Though many skiers still do not like the idea of sharing slopes with snowboarders, it has become common to see boarders at most major ski resorts throughout the world. Snowboarding is accepted now more than ever, with over 5 million winter sports fans hitting the slopes every year. Look out, skiers! Snowboarding is here to stay.

_____ 1. Before the second step of the snowboard, Burchett's snowboard had been the basic model for more than _____ years.

(A) ten　　　　　(B) thirty　　　　(C) forty　　　　(D) eighty

_____ 2. Snowboarding has been really popular among winter sports lovers since _____ .

(A) the early 1990s　　　　　　(B) the late 1960s

(C) 1965　　　　　　　　　　　(D) 1938

_____ 3. Poppen made the "Snurfer" by _____ .

(A) using a piece of plywood and trying to secure his feet with some clothesline

(B) binding two pieces of hardwood and tying a string to the front end

(C) binding two skis together and tying a rope to the front end

(D) gluing some cardboard onto the top of plywood

_____ 4. What does the last sentence in this passage mean?

(A) Snowboarding has been generally and permanently accepted.

(B) Snowboarding equipment can be more expensive.

(C) Snowboarding is as dangerous as skiing.

(D) Go snowboarding and stay young.

_____ 5. According to the passage, which of the following is NOT true?

(A) The Snurfer was the first marketed snowboard.

(B) Now most of the winter resorts do not accept snowboarders.

(C) The Snurfer was first made by Poppen as a toy for his daughter.

(D) In 1998, snowboarding was first introduced at the Winter Olympics.

Unit 09

Alien Accidents?

In July of 1947, in New Mexico desert, a rancher found a large amount of unusual debris scattered over an area that was about three quarters of a mile long and several hundred feet wide. He reported the incident to the U.S. Air Force at Roswell. They soon started an investigation and issued a news release, saying that they found a crashed flying saucer and alien bodies. The nation was shocked by the news.

However, four hours after this first announcement, the story was changed: now what was thought to have been a flying saucer was actually a weather balloon. Because the U.S. government first admitted to have found alien bodies and later denied it, more people began to believe that it was true and that the government was trying to hide something.

The case was finally closed fifty years later when the U.S. government confirmed that the so-called alien bodies were test dummies used in a top-secret research program. Whatever the case, UFO mania began and reported sightings of UFOs became a part of popular culture. UFOs were thought to be responsible for many mysterious things, such as crop circles and even disappearances in the Bermuda Triangle.

Many people believe UFOs and aliens are real, and they also believe there must be some possibility of intelligent life out there. Other people tend to be doubtful without any concrete proof. Unfortunately, if there is any evidence of the existence of UFOs or aliens, it is kept from the public. Do you believe in their existence? The answer is up in the air until we have better and more reliable evidence.

_____ 1. What's the main idea of this passage?

  (A) The general public believe that the U.S. government lied about the Roswell incident.

  (B) The Roswell incident aroused a great public interest in the actual existence of UFOs.

  (C) The majority of people think that aliens and UFOs do exist.

  (D) It is believed that the Bermuda Triangle was a trap made by aliens.

_____ 2. When did the U.S. Air Force issue a "case-closed" report stating that the so-called "alien bodies" were test dummies?

  (A) In 1947.　(B) In 1974.　(C) In 1994.　(D) In 1997.

_____ 3. According to the passage, which of the following is true about the Roswell incident?

  (A) A UFO crashed in a New Mexico river in July, 1947.

  (B) A rancher found alien bodies and reported them to the Air Force.

  (C) Soon after the incident was reported, the government began to investigate it.

  (D) The first announcement the Air Force made was that the so-called alien bodies were just military dummies.

_____ 4. The U.S. government's attitude towards the Roswell incident made more people believe that the government intended to _____ .

  (A) cover up the truth and hide what had been found out

  (B) protect American people from being attacked by aliens

  (C) disclose their great findings

  (D) suggest that an extraterrestrial life form actually exists

_____ 5. What might be the author's attitude towards the existence of UFO and aliens?

  (A) Positive.　　(B) Indifferent.　　(C) Doubtful.　　(D) Neutral.

Unit 10

Spain's Tomatina Festival

On the last Wednesday of every August, tens of thousands of people fill the streets of Buñol, Spain to celebrate the Tomatina Festival.

There are at least two stories about its origin. In one story, there was a man who played music very poorly, and his friends decided to play a joke by throwing tomatoes at him. In the other story, which is considered to be a more reliable and accurate version, some young people in 1945 took tomatoes from vegetable vendors in the town square and used **them** in a fight just for fun.

These young people gathered the following year on the same day, bringing their tomatoes to fight again. The police stopped them, and the town refused to permit the tomato fight until 1950. It then had to be stopped again, owing to attacks on other people who refused to take part in it. By 1959, the people of Buñol asked the Town Hall to allow the festival to take place; this time, some rules were made to avoid accidents and attacks. The local government wanted to make sure the festival maintained its spirit of fun.

The rules are still in effect today, and they have proved to be an effective way to prevent injuries. For example, participants mustn't tear other people's clothing, mustn't throw any tomato after the festival is over, and mustn't bring bottles or other objects that could be dangerous. Of course, the most important rule is that all of the tomatoes must be crushed before they're thrown into the air, so that they won't hurt anyone.

Without the Tomatina Festival, few people would have ever heard of the town Buñol. Today, people travel from all over the world just to take part in this unusual and unforgettable event.

_____ 1. The Tomatina Festival was finally given official recognition in _____ and continues to be held every year till now.

(A) 1950   (B) 1945   (C) 1959   (D) 1969

_____ 2. The pronoun "them" in the second paragraph refers to _____ .

(A) young people   (B) tomatoes

(C) vendors   (D) versions

_____ 3. The passage is most likely taken from a(n) _____ .

(A) agriculture magazine   (B) travel magazine

(C) history report   (D) consumer guide

_____ 4. It can be inferred that the festival was not allowed to take place for several years because _____ .

(A) tomatoes were in short supply

(B) the local people would attack strangers

(C) the town hall would get too dirty to be cleaned

(D) the authorities feared that it would get out of control

_____ 5. According to the passage, which of the following is NOT true?

(A) The festival is held on the last Wednesday in August in Buñol, Spain.

(B) Participants must stop throwing tomatoes as soon as the end is announced.

(C) The festival is not only held for fun but also for its religious significance.

(D) It is generally thought that the festival dates back to 1945, when a fight among young men broke out in the town square.

Talking Back?

We normally don't like it if we are talked back to. We make an exception, however, for our parrots.

Parrots are famous for having the ability to talk, but actually they have no vocal cords. Instead, they have longer and more muscular tongues than other birds, which can be important in modifying sounds. They control their throat muscles to push their tongues backwards and forwards and thus produce sounds. It's interesting to find that parrots make sounds like "ee" by opening their beaks wider. Although parrots can speak a few sentences with words in the right order, they are not able to use syntax as humans do. As a result, they are not generally considered to have the real ability to talk.

Still, many scientists and pet owners think that when parrots are talking, they are communicating with people. Professor Irene Pepperberg has worked with parrots and believes in their intelligence. She claims that some parrots' intelligence can **rival** that of a human child between the ages of 3 and 5. Take her oldest African Grey, Alex, for example. Over the last 27 years, she has been teaching him to do some complex tasks. He can talk with a vocabulary of 100 words and can even think. The professor says Alex's actions are not just an instinctive response but a result of reasoning and choice. In addition, he can identify colors and shapes, and recognize 50 different objects. He also knows the concepts of sameness and difference.

If you want to teach parrots to talk, remember parrots learn to talk through one-on-one relationship with their owners. Having a good relationship with parrots is always helpful in training them to speak. Try to establish a verbal routine with them. Praise also does wonders to keep parrots talking.

_____ 1. Which of the following is NOT what parrots use when they make sounds?

(A) The vocal cord.   (B) The throat.

(C) The tongue.   (D) The beak.

_____ 2. Some people think that parrots are unable to really talk because _____ .

(A) they cannot say a complete sentence

(B) they are unlikely to talk in the complex form of human language

(C) they cannot make a sound in the same way that humans do

(D) humans do not like being talked back to

_____ 3. According to the passage, which of the following is NOT true about Alex?

(A) He has been taught by Irene Pepperberg for more than 20 years.

(B) He cannot seperate objects of the same color or shape into a group.

(C) He can respond to his owner's orders and perform certain tasks.

(D) His actions are based on reasoning.

_____ 4. When teaching parrots to speak, owners are advised to avoid _____ .

(A) teaching two parrots at a time

(B) establishing a good relationship with them

(C) rewarding them for their good performance

(D) saying "good morning" to them at the beginning of each day

_____ 5. The word "rival" in the 3rd paragraph can be best replaced by "_____ ."

(A) hit   (B) honor

(C) equal   (D) worsen

Unit 12

Blogging for Good

Of the 38 million blogs in cyberspace, 52.8% of them are set up and maintained by teenagers. What can be seen in teens' blogs? Maybe his or her artwork, stories about school, favorite songs and movies, complaints, and random thoughts about life. In short, blogs can be just about anything that teens use to communicate themselves to others.

Teenage bloggers use their websites for self-expression and to reach out to friends, family and the outside world. By revealing themselves online, teens are searching for others like them. They try to find a sense of belonging.

Many people believe that online diaries actually serve some good. For instance, blogging seems to boost literacy. Isn't a teenager who updates his or her blog every day really writing a daily essay? That could definitely do wonders for his or her writing skills. Besides, teenagers can also acquire a sense of satisfaction from expressing themselves. Another example of the far-reaching effects of blogging is how it brings social awareness to teenagers. Some of them not only post personal experience on the web, but also encourage other teens to go out and get involved with activities against world hunger, child labor, and so on. What's more, by reading their children's daily postings, parents can get to know their **offspring** better. A blog is certainly more revealing than awkward dinner conversations.

Parents and teachers may be right: blogging can be dangerous. Yet, it can help today's youths in numerous ways, which may push all of us to have teens blogging for good.

_____ 1. What's the main idea of this passage?

(A) Blogs have exploded in popularity among teens.

(B) Blogging is a form of self-therapy for teens.

(C) Blogging helps teens create and maintain their social ties.

(D) Teens flock to blogs and they benefit a lot from them.

_____ 2. Which of the following benefits of teen blogging is NOT stated in this passage?

(A) Expanding teens' view of the future.

(B) Enhancing teens' ability to write.

(C) Developing teens' social awareness.

(D) Getting a sense of satisfaction.

_____ 3. Which of the following is NOT stated in this passage as teenagers' purpose of using blogs?

(A) Expressing themselves.

(B) Connecting with others.

(C) Showing off their technology skills.

(D) Searching for identity.

_____ 4. The word "offspring" in the 3rd paragraph can be replaced by "_____."

(A) teenagers   (B) laborers

(C) bloggers   (D) children

_____ 5. What is the author' attitude toward teenage bloggers?

(A) For them.   (B) Against them.

(C) Neutral.   (D) Indifferent.

Unit 13

Laughter is the Best Medicine

A recent study performed at the University of Maryland showed that laughing may help prevent heart disease. The researchers found that people with heart disease are less likely to laugh in a variety of situations compared with people of the same age without heart disease.

However, these researchers don't know yet why laughing protects the heart. Maybe it is because laughing releases protective chemicals in our bodies, or because it exercises our hearts and lungs and thus increases the amount of oxygen in our blood. Dr. Miller, the leader of the team, said, "We know that exercising will reduce the risk of heart disease. Perhaps regular, hearty laughter should be added to the list."

Another benefit of laughter is that it boosts the immune system by increasing the number of T-cells, which attack viruses, foreign cells and cancer cells. Also, it increases B-cells, which produce disease-destroying antibodies. Laughter can also lower blood pressure, and stress can drain away as a result.

It is also believed that laughter helps patients who are undergoing painful procedures or who suffer from pain-expectation anxiety. This is because laughter causes the release of the body's natural pain killers and thus provides a temporary **distraction** from pain. Some children's hospitals are using professional clown doctors to go into children's wards and inject a bit of fun. They are not doctors but actors dressed as clowns. They do a very simple job but have a very positive impact. Laughing not only costs nothing to provide positive benefits to our health, but also has no negative side effects.

_____ **1.** The main purpose of this passage is to _____ .
  (A) explore Dr. Miller's theory about laughter
  (B) explain laughter's effect on pain
  (C) explain the benefits of laughter to health
  (D) describe how stress influences our health

_____ **2.** What do clown doctors do in children's hospitals?
  (A) They help doctors with painful treatments.
  (B) They help nurses give sick children some injections.
  (C) They give talks on the benefits of laughter to children's parents.
  (D) They use their skills to treat sick children with laughter.

_____ **3.** Dr. Miller and his team members found that _____ .
  (A) laughter helps relax tense muscles
  (B) stress appears to be our number one killer
  (C) laughter allows a person to "forget" about pain
  (D) people with heart disease generally laugh less

_____ **4.** The word "distraction" in the 4th paragraph means something that

  _____ .
  (A) turns people's attention away   (B) can be added to the total
  (C) makes people worried   (D) people are content with

_____ **5.** According to the passage, which of the following is NOT true?
  (A) Dr. Miller clearly understands why laughter helps prevent heart disease.
  (B) There are no known negative side effects of laughter.
  (C) Laughter brings about an increase in the number of cells that can attack
     viruses.
  (D) To have a healthy heart, we should exercise regularly and laugh more.

The Coca-Cola Company

Coca-Cola is the world's most popular soft drink. The company can be characterized by its genius in promoting its products **coupled** with its drive to continually expand its markets.

Coca-Cola was being promoted by an advertisement in a local American newspaper in as early as 1886, just a few months after its original formula had been invented by John Pemberton, an Atlanta pharmacist. He marketed Coca-Cola as a tonic drink to cure headaches, but the slogan was effective and simple: "Drink Coca-Cola."

Nationwide expansion followed the formation of the Coca-Cola Company in 1892. The company established bottling factories outside Atlanta, enabling the consumption of Coca-Cola to spread to every U.S. state. This expansion was accompanied by Coca-Cola advertisements on barn doors and the sides of buildings throughout America, and by hiring famous singers, actors and sports stars to promote Coca-Cola. Specially made Coca-Cola calendars, trays and bottles also helped establish the brand name.

In the twentieth century, Coca-Cola expanded internationally. Since the 1920s, the company has bombarded people with the image of the Coca-Cola trademark from electric signs in cities around the world. Coca-Cola took advantage of **the new mass media**, advertised on radio and TV, and created slogans such as "Coke Is It!" (1982). In 1971 Coca-Cola's global ambitions were captured in a famous TV ad which showed a large crowd of young people of different races gathering on a hilltop, singing "I'd Like to Buy the World a Coke." The company has also sponsored major sporting events such as the Olympic Games and the FIFA World Cup.

The company has maintained its drive and vision, and continues in pursuit of new markets to ensure that Coca-Cola is "around the corner from everywhere."

_____ 1. The passage is written mainly to describe _____.
(A) why people around the world love Coca-Cola
(B) how Coca-Cola was accidentally invented
(C) how Coca-Cola has been successfully promoted and marketed
(D) why the slogans created by the company have attracted consumers'
interest

_____ 2. Coca-Cola's original formula _____.
(A) was invented by a local newspaperman
(B) had a medical effect
(C) was invented in 1892
(D) was popular worldwide immediately

_____ 3. Which of the following is NOT described as a reason why Coca-Cola was
able to spread everywhere in the U.S. before the 1920s?
(A) Bottling factories were established outside Atlanta.
(B) A lot of celebrities helped promote Coca-Cola.
(C) Coca-Cola was promoted through electric advertising signs.
(D) Consumers around the nation loved its specially made products.

_____ 4. The word "coupled" in the 1st paragraph can be best replaced by
"_____."
(A) conveyed   (B) combined
(C) compared   (D) filled

_____ 5. The words "the new mass media" in the 4th paragraph refer to _____.
(A) TV and the Internet   (B) radio and outdoor advertising
(C) radio and newspapers   (D) radio and TV

Unit 15

Therapy Animals

Therapy animals, also called therapy pets, are mostly dogs, but can include cats, rabbits, or even birds. Certain personality traits are important for being capable therapy animals. They need to like people and be gentle, controllable, and most importantly, have a stable personality. These basic traits enable therapy animals to be quiet and patient while people are petting or touching them.

These **short interactions** between people and animals can have a positive impact on a person's health. Although there is no data from laboratories that shows how interacting with an animal can physically help people, scientific studies show that people report feeling less lonely and less depressed after visiting a therapy animal.

Generally speaking, nursing homes and hospitals are common places for animal therapy programs because elderly people or patients often get lonely in these places. Therapy animals' visits are usually scheduled for once or twice a week, and the residents normally look forward to these visits, which are often the highlight of their week. Some hospitals also have such programs to arrange animals to spend some time with long-term patients or with those who are terminally ill. Elderly people and patients benefit from contact with therapy animals, making them feel more physically healthy, more hopeful and less lonely.

The animals involved in the programs, however, are not usually owned by a therapy pet organization. The people who own these special animals are usually volunteers who want to help the elderly and the sick. Before being part of these programs, pets must be evaluated by certain organizations. If these pets are found to be appropriate, they will be given official authorization to join an animal therapy program.

_____ 1. What's the main idea of this passage?

    (A) Therapy animals can help sick and elderly people feel healthier and less lonely.

    (B) Most nursing homes and hospitals have therapy animal programs.

    (C) In addition to cats and dogs, rabbits and birds can also be used as therapy animals.

    (D) More and more organizations are being established to train therapy animals.

_____ 2. Which of the following is NOT a trait that good therapy animals need?

    (A) Friendly.   (B) Patient.   (C) Moody.   (D) Gentle.

_____ 3. The phrase "short interactions" in the 2nd paragraph refers to _____.

    (A) chatting or touching   (B) petting or touching

    (C) gazing or petting   (D) visiting or nursing

_____ 4. In can be inferred from this passage that _____.

    (A) dogs are the best therapy animal

    (B) therapy pets' success depends on their owners

    (C) pets bring the most benefits to mentally ill patients

    (D) therapy pets are a source of expectation and hope

_____ 5. According to the passage, which of the following is true?

    (A) Badly behaved but friendly pets are welcomed in therapy programs.

    (B) Residents in nursing homes and patients in hospitals have everyday visits from therapy pets.

    (C) Any therapy animal should first be evaluated before becoming involved in an animal therapy program.

    (D) All of the pets used in therapy programs are owned by organizations.

The Food and Philosophy of Veganism

There are many reasons why people go on a vegan diet. Some of these people are concerned with the ethics of eating animals, while others are worried about their health. On the ethical side, the mistreatment of food animals is well known. This is also true for animals on which cosmetics and soaps are sometimes tested. In addition, there is the issue of the large amount of natural resources it takes to raise animals for food. It is better for the environment if people can only grow and eat fruits, vegetables and grains.

On the health side, fitness-conscious vegans know that eating natural vegetables, fruits, nuts and whole grains can be very good for their health. They point out that not eating animal products makes them feel they have more energy and strength. Some scientific evidence supports this by showing that eating a lot of meat can be unhealthy because of all the artificial drugs used in raising food animals on large farms.

Can a vegan diet, itself, be unhealthy? After all, isn't the practice of not eating any animal products dangerous? Not necessarily. A carefully planned vegan diet offers all the nutrients the body needs. Potential problems with a vegan diet include not getting enough iron and calcium, which typically come from meat and dairy products. However, by eating plenty of grains, beans and green vegetables, one can be sure to get **these important nutrients**. In addition, because most people's protein comes from eating meat, vegans must be especially careful to ensure they are getting enough protein. Good sources of non-meat protein include nuts, peanut butter, tofu, soymilk and oats.

_____ 1. Which of the following reasons for veganism is NOT stated in this passage?

(A) Health.   (B) Animal rights.

(C) Religion.   (D) Environment.

_____ 2. Which of the following food is NOT eaten or used by vegans?

(A) Grains.   (B) Vegetables.

(C) Leather.   (D) Soymilk.

_____ 3. The phrase "these important nutrients" in the 3rd paragraph refers to

_____ .

(A) protein and calcium   (B) iron and calcium

(C) iron and zinc   (D) protein and iron

_____ 4. According to the passage, sometimes vegans do not use certain cosmetics and soaps because _____ .

(A) they have been tested on animals

(B) they are derived from animal products

(C) they pollute our environment

(D) they cause skin allergies

_____ 5. The passage was written mainly to _____ .

(A) compare   (B) entertain

(C) criticize   (D) inform

Living Below Sea Level

Sitting between Lake Pontchartrain and the Mississippi River near the Gulf of Mexico, New Orleans was once a thriving U.S. city, famous for its Mardi Gras celebrations and talented jazz artists. Before Hurricane Katrina flooded the city in 2005, almost half a million people had enjoyed the city's relaxing culture.

New Orleans rests in a bowl about two meters below sea level, and it is protected from the water around it by a system of levees, which dates back to the 1960s. These levees, or water barriers, circle the entire city and prevent the waters of Lake Pontchartrain and the Mississippi River from rushing into the city. Some levees are made of concrete, but many are made of earth, reaching 210 kilometers around the city. Within these levees are pumping stations and canals to keep the land dry, even after heavy rainfall.

In 2005, Hurricane Katrina hit New Orleans at full force. Katrina's high winds and storm surge destroyed some levees. As a result, more than 80 percent of the city was left completely underwater, killing more than 1500 people and leaving hundreds of thousands of people homeless and thousands without food, fresh water or electricity. To make things worse, the major roads going in and out of the city were either destroyed or under water, making it very difficult for survivors to leave the city or for aid workers to enter the city.

To help these people and their city, the federal and local government have spent hundred billion dollars cleaning up the mess, building better levees and rebuilding damaged homes and businesses. The extent of the damage, however, was so severe that some experts estimated that it would take more than ten years for the city to recover and for all its former population to return.

_____ 1. Which of the following is NOT what New Orleans relies on to keep the city from being filled with water?

(A) Levees.   (B) Pumping stations.

(C) Canals.   (D) Water Dams.

_____ 2. Before Hurricane Katrina hit New Orleans, the system of levees worked fairly well for about _____ .

(A) 45 years   (B) 65 years

(C) 86 years   (D) 100 years

_____ 3. New Orleans sits below sea level in a bowl bordered by _____ .

(A) the Mississippi River and the Gulf of Mexico

(B) the Mississippi River and Lake Pontchartrain

(C) the Gulf of Mexico and Lake Pontchartrain

(D) Lake Pontchartrain and the Atlantic Ocean

_____ 4. New Orleans' former population was about _____ .

(A) 300,000   (B) 400,000

(C) 500,000   (D) 1,000,000

_____ 5. According to the passage, which of the following is true?

(A) Hurricane Katrina left the city completely underwater.

(B) Hurricane Katrina killed hundreds of residents.

(C) It would take five years to repair all of the damage caused by Katrina.

(D) The city was so seriously damaged that getting into it to rescue the victims became very difficult.

Velcro: the Wonder Fastener

The hook and loop fastener, also called Velcro, is a very important invention that plays a major part in most of our lives. These fasteners are used to join various materials together, such as cloth, plastics, leather, etc. The idea of this invention actually came from nature.

The first hook and loop fastener was invented by George de Mestral, a keen nature observer. He observed that thorny seed-bearing sacs used to get attached to his woolen clothes and the fur coat of his dog. Wondering why these burrs attached so strongly to his clothes, he observed them under the microscope and found out that **they** had numerous tiny hooks that could **adhere** to the woolen fibers of his clothes. This encouraged him to try and create similar material that could be used as a fastener.

He believed that he could make a fastener that would use the same principle as natural burrs: a series of hooks that would hold firm on a layer of numerous fuzzy fibers. He then worked with many textile makers and succeeded in making the first hook and loop fastener out of cotton material. His fastener had two separate parts: one had numerous tiny hooks, and the other had smooth and fuzzy fibers. When they were joined together, the fuzzy fibers would get firmly caught in the hooks, which held them securely close. Even though the initial fastener was not strong enough for all purposes, the quality of the fasteners was improved by making them from a variety of other materials.

The name Velcro was derived from the French words *Velour* for velvet, and *Crochet*, for hook. The name came to be associated with hook and loop fasteners because Mestral named his company Velcro. Whatever the name is, Velcro is now considered as an unavoidable necessity because of its strength and convenience.

_____ 1. What's the main idea of this passage?

(A) Nature is regarded as the best inventor of all.

(B) George de Mestral loved two things: inventing and the outdoors.

(C) Velcro was invented by George de Mestral, who got his idea from nature.

(D) Velcro, the wonder fastener, can now be found in countless applications.

_____ 2. The pronoun "they" in the 2nd paragraph refers to _____.

(A) clothes   (B) fibers

(C) visits   (D) burrs

_____ 3. The word "adhere" in the 2nd paragraph can be best replaced by "_____."

(A) observe   (B) stick

(C) improve   (D) loop

_____ 4. What material was Mestral's first hook and loop fastener made of?

(A) Fur.   (B) Cotton.

(C) Leather.   (D) Plastics.

_____ 5. According to the passage, which of the following is NOT true?

(A) Mestral named his invention "Velcro" after two French words.

(B) Velcro is actually the name of Mestral's fastener company.

(C) Mestral worked alone and finally made the first hook and loop fastener.

(D) After a lot of improvements, the fastener is strong enough to fasten a variety of objects.

Unit 19

Finding Ancient Beasts

Woolly mammoths are extinct elephant-like animals with long curved tusks and a covering of long and dense hair. They lived in the northern regions of the world, such as Europe and northern America.

The word "woolly" means "hairy." "Mammoth" is based on a Tartar word meaning "earth," because the people who found mammoths centuries ago thought the creatures lived underground. Although the English language now includes "mammoth" to mean "very large," woolly mammoths were not really very large. They weighed 6 to 8 tons and were up to four meters tall.

What is special about these extinct animals? Many mammoths' fossils and remains have been found, compared to other ancient animals. What's more, no other ancient animals, such as dinosaurs, have ever been found frozen. Thirty-nine frozen mammoth bodies have been discovered, but only four are complete. These frozen bodies are perfect for scientists to do DNA tests on to understand more about them.

More than 26,000 years ago, about 100 woolly mammoths were trapped and died in a pond near what is now the southwest edge of Hot Springs, South Dakota. They were found by chance in 1974. Now the Mammoth Site is the world's largest concentration of woolly mammoth bones ever discovered. Visitors can actually go into large dry sink holes and see the skeletons, which remain as they were found.

The information scientists have gained from studying mammoths is valuable for learning about elephant genetics. In addition, they can learn more about what the planet was like thousands of years ago and understand what climate changes led to the mammoths' extinction.

_____ 1. Which of the following is NOT what makes woolly mammoths special?

(A) No other ancient animals have been found frozen.

(B) Woolly mammoths are the tallest extinct animals.

(C) Scientists can do DNA tests on the frozen mammoths.

(D) More remains of woolly mammoths have been found than those of other extinct animals.

_____ 2. Scientists can learn the following information from studying mammoths EXCEPT _____.

(A) the causes of mammoths' extinction

(B) elephant genetics

(C) what the earth was like centuries ago

(D) the real meaning of "mammoth"

_____ 3. Woolly mammoths did NOT live in _____.

(A) Northern America   (B) Northern Canada

(C) New Zealand   (D) Europe

_____ 4. Which of the following is NOT true about the Mammoth Site?

(A) Visitors can go into large holes to see the skeletons.

(B) The mammoth bones are displayed in the exhibit windows.

(C) These mammoths died over 26,000 years ago.

(D) These skeletons were accidentally discovered.

_____ 5. "Mammoth" means "earth" in the Tartan language and was used because of the long-held belief that _____.

(A) mammoths once roamed the earth

(B) mammoths were fed on earth

(C) mammoths were the oldest species on earth

(D) mammoths lived underground

Farris Hassan's Bogus Adventure?

Here's Farris Hassan's story: In December 2005, he decided to write an essay for his high school journalism class, in which the writer had to experience first-hand what he or she reported. Hassan wanted to record how the Iraq war was affecting the people in Iraq. So, without telling anyone, he bought a plane ticket and took off for the Middle East.

When word about the bold youngster reached the press, Farris Hassan's unbelievable adventure was reported around the world. Journalists told about how he eventually arrived in Iraq and how he ran into trouble on his journey. Although he looked like an Iraqi, he couldn't speak Arabic. The media and most of the world **hailed** Farris Hassan as a hero.

Many people were amazed at how an ordinary teenager could have the guts to make such a dangerous journey by himself. As the press continued to praise Hassan after his adventure, some journalists thought the story seemed "too good to be true" and started investigating Hassan and his trip to Iraq.

Reporters discovered that Farris Hassan came from a rich family. They also learned that both his parents were doctors, and that he went to a private high school. The media also found out that Farris had never enrolled in any journalism class and that his school didn't even offer one. Worse, his father apparently knew about the trip before he left and helped him arrange the airline ticket and traveling visa.

Many in the press now consider Hassan's trip to be just a schoolboy prank. But why would anyone go through the trouble to do such a thing? It is hard to imagine what Farris was hoping to gain, other than being known as a liar for the rest of his life.

_____ 1. Hassan's excuse for his trip to Iraq was that he wanted to _____.

(A) visit his parents' friends

(B) better understand the Iraq war

(C) put his journalism lessons into practice

(D) uncover what the U.S. Army did in Iraq

_____ 2. Why did some journalists decide to investigate Hassan and his trip?

(A) Because he had special family background.

(B) Because he was not given the school assignment.

(C) Because he couldn't speak Arabic.

(D) Because his story was too perfect.

_____ 3. Hassan was able to leave his home alone and arrive safely in Iraq with the

help of _____.

(A) his mother   (B) his father

(C) his school principal   (D) some journalists

_____ 4. Hassan's story quickly caught the attention of the media because

_____.

(A) they admired the teen's courage to set out on such a journey on his own

(B) they were amazed at the way he spoke

(C) they were surprised at the teen's attitude towards the Iraqi people

(D) they were curious about how he looked at the Iraq war

_____ 5. The word "hailed" in the 2nd paragraph can be best replaced by

"_____."

(A) called   (B) connected

(C) recognized   (D) despised

Unit 21

Eva Peron

Eva Peron was born in 1919 in the small town of Los Toldos, Argentina. As the daughter of a rancher and his mistress, Eva lived under a cloud of injustice, uncertainty and poverty. Her father died when she was seven. She and her family had to survive by working as cooks for wealthy families. The beautiful teenaged Eva dreamed of escaping her difficult environment.

When she was just fifteen, Eva ran away to Buenos Aires, Argentina's capital city. There she met a number of powerful suitors, who helped her find acting jobs in radio soap operas and the movies. She finally worked her way up the ladder of success through a series of affairs with **them**. Eva achieved prosperity but not the fame she really wanted, so she decided to turn her ambitions to politics. When she was twenty-five, she started dating Juan Peron, an army officer. The ambitious couple were well suited for each other and quickly married in 1945.

In the next year, Juan was elected President, and Eva became the First Lady, the most powerful woman in Argentina. However, she hadn't forgotten her background, and she used her influence to build hospitals, schools and homes for the poor and elderly. As a result, Eva became extremely popular with ordinary people. Yet, she had many enemies. The upper class was jealous of her high social position, accusing her of using men to "sleep her way to power." Eva also showed the dark side of her personality by refusing to respect the human rights of her opponents. She had many people imprisoned, and supported her husband's increasing use of military power to control the country.

Suddenly, in 1951, tragedy struck. Eva developed cancer and died the following year at just 33. However, Eva Peron had achieved her life's goal——she had become, and remains, the most famous woman in Argentinian history.

_____ 1. Eva achieved her first success in life as a(n) _____ .

    (A) cook   (B) actress

    (C) social worker   (D) defender of human rights

_____ 2. The pronoun "them" in the 2nd paragraph refers to _____ .

    (A) jobs   (B) movies

    (C) suitors   (D) the press

_____ 3. The passage was written to _____ .

    (A) provide a brief biography of Eva Peron

    (B) show how Eva took advantage of her power

    (C) describe how Eva defended human rights

    (D) explain why Eva went into politics

_____ 4. According to the passage, which of the following is true?

    (A) Eva was a devil in the eyes of all Argentines.

    (B) Eva treated her opponents unjustly and cruelly.

    (C) Eva lived very happily in her childhood.

    (D) Eva died of cancer in 1951.

_____ 5. Eva was adored by common people in Argentina because _____ .

    (A) she was a fascinating and complex woman

    (B) she came from a poverty-stricken area

    (C) she was devoted to helping the poor and the old

    (D) she was the wife of the most powerful man in the country

Wait a Minute! I Never Bought That!

Imagine that one day you get an angry phone call from an electronics store, demanding that you pay thousands of dollars in bills for an expensive refrigerator. The only problem is, you've never bought anything from that store! Obviously, you have been the victim of identity theft, the fastest growing crime in the world. Identity theft occurs when thieves steal your personal information and pretend to be you, usually so that they can buy expensive things or commit other forms of **fraud**. Identity theft is often invisible, and the damage **it** causes can take years to fix.

Identity theft is spreading quickly for many reasons. First, people resist laws that would make credit cards safer. They prefer convenience to safety. Second, the growing popularity of Internet shopping has created new dangers. Thieves can steal your information easily through fake web pages, emails, and other tricks. Later, they can sign back on to the Internet and anonymously buy things online, without the risk of using a fake card in person. Third, because of the Internet and cell phones, identity thieves can steal personal information from people in different countries, making them almost impossible to be found and arrested.

The good news is that there are several easy things you can do to protect yourself. If you get a strange call from a bank or company asking you for information, just hang up. Then check the company's published number or web page, and request to speak to its service department. That way you can be sure the person you are talking to is not a fraud. Also, be sure you shred all documents before putting them in the trash. Finally, don't forget to check your credit reports and immediately report any suspicious charges.

_____ **1.** Identity theft occurs when _____ .

    (A) a thief breaks into someone's house and steals personal information

    (B) a thief steals and uses a person's personal data to commit a crime

    (C) someone tries to break into computer systems to spread virus

    (D) a person threatens another person through the Internet

_____ **2.** Which word in this passage is closest in meaning to "fraud"?

    (A) Convenience.   (B) Charge.

    (C) Popularity.   (D) Cheat.

_____ **3.** What is the author's purpose in mentioning "Also, be sure you shred all documents before putting them in the trash."?

    (A) To warn that thieves might get personal information from trash.

    (B) To provide a good way of collecting trash.

    (C) To discuss problems about documents and trash.

    (D) To explain why documents are important.

_____ **4.** Which of the following is NOT stated in this passage?

    (A) Criminals can steal information through fake web pages.

    (B) The problem of identity theft is spreading beyond national borders.

    (C) Online shopping makes it easier to steal useful information.

    (D) Criminals will steal bank or credit card statements from mailboxes.

_____ **5.** The pronoun "it" in the 1st paragraph refers to _____ .

    (A) personal information   (B) damage

    (C) identity theft   (D) problem

Animal Alerts

In 1975, a 7.3-magnitude earthquake hit Haicheng, China. A few days before the quake, city officials had already ordered an evacuation. This was done after local people reported seeing snakes emerging from hibernation during the winter and freezing to death on the roads. The quake would have killed 100,000 people if the city had been full. In 2004, two panic-stricken elephants at Khao Lak were seen breaking free from their chains and running for higher ground just five minutes before the place was destroyed by a massive tsunami. Some confused people followed and saved themselves.

People have observed animals doing some scary and peculiar things before natural disasters. Dogs, for example, will howl continuously. Pigs will start biting other pigs. Bees will suddenly flee their hives. Walking around as if they were dizzy, mice can easily be caught by hand, which is lucky for them because cats will be hiding.

Wildlife experts believe that animals are better equipped than humans to sense changes in their surroundings. Their sensitive hearing is very different from that of humans. Tsunamis may cause sound waves that travel faster through rock formations beneath the sea floor than on the water's surface. Elephants can hear **them** first and have time to flee. Researchers also indicate that many animals can feel seismic waves or changes in electricity in the air before an earthquake.

Even though we cannot actually prove that animals can sense natural disasters, it is difficult to ignore their alerting abilities. So be on guard when homing pigeons lose their way or when fish start jumping out of water. If we cannot be as watchful as animals, we should at least watch them!

_____ 1. Which of the following might be the message those Haicheng residents got
from city officials before the earthquake happened?
(A) "Hide up or they will find you."　(B) "Tidy up or you will get ill."
(C) "Watch out or you will get hurt."　(D) "Move out or you will die."

_____ 2. Which of the following is believed by researchers to be one of the reasons
animals can "predict" earthquakes?
(A) Animals can see the changes on the earth caused by quakes.
(B) Animals can hear sound waves from the collapsing of buildings.
(C) Animals can feel the earth's vibrations or changes in electricity in the air.
(D) Animals can smell seismic waves of earthquakes.

_____ 3. Which of the following best describes the author's attitude toward using
animals as natural disaster detectors?
(A) Most scientists disagree with the idea that animal behaviors can be used
to predict natural disasters.
(B) Animals survive by being alert, and humans should find clues from them.
(C) There has been no evidence as to animals' abilities to sense earthquakes.
(D) Animals often die during natural disasters despite their keen senses.

_____ 4. The pronoun "them" in the 3rd paragraph refers to _____ .
(A) rock formations　(B) sound waves　(C) humans　(D) surroundings

_____ 5. What specific animal behavior was observed before the quake hit Haicheng?
(A) Snakes crawled out from their winter sleep.
(B) Dogs howled continuously.
(C) Fish jumped out of water.
(D) Bees fled their hives.

The Problems with Spam

Do you feel like you're getting too many email advertisements? These unwanted electronic messages, often called "spam," account for up to half of all email sent and received worldwide. Getting rid of these messages costs companies billions of dollars every year, as their employees waste valuable time deleting messages. Even more costly, companies must spend millions of dollars on software that helps catch and **filter** spam messages before they reach company computers.

Not only does spam waste time and money, but it also can be harmful. Some spam messages hide "spyware," which is the computer software that can get secret or personal information from computers. Other spam may contain "viruses," which are also hidden software programs that use other people's emails to send spam, or that provide information to help thieves or hackers find a way into computers. Some computer viruses simply erase everything in a computer, making it useless and destroying valuable information.

Unfortunately, little can be done to reduce the amount of spam being sent. When any software is developed to block spam, the people who send spam can just find a way to bypass these blocks. Governments also seem powerless to control spam, because the Internet is international, and anti-spam laws in one country don't always apply in another. It also seems that whenever someone who sends spam is arrested, another takes his or her place.

Even though spam is a serious problem, there are still ways to protect yourself and your computer from it. Never open an email attachment if you don't know the sender. Don't post your email address publicly on any web page. Share your primary e-mail address only with people you know.

_____ 1. Which of the following best describes what spam is?

(A) Spam contains email messages.

(B) Spam is an email software.

(C) Spam is the Internet version of postal junk mail.

(D) Spam is a free web-based email service.

_____ 2. The second paragraph is mainly about _____ .

(A) information about spyware

(B) what computer hackers are doing

(C) loss of valuable information

(D) viruses and spyware that spam spreads

_____ 3. Which of the following is NOT mentioned in this passage as a cause of why the amount of spam cannot be greatly reduced?

(A) No anti-spam software is 100 percent effective.

(B) It's impossible to arrest all the spammers.

(C) Spammers always buy lists of email addresses from other spammers.

(D) Spam is a worldwide problem; one country's anti-spam laws don't necessarily apply in another.

_____ 4. Which of the following is NOT mentioned as a way to avoid spam?

(A) Create a secure email password.

(B) Never post your email address publicly online.

(C) Never open an email attachment sent by someone you don't know.

(D) Don't give your primary email address to anyone you don't know.

_____ 5. The word "filter" in the 1st paragraph can be best replaced by " _____ ."

(A) retain   (B) remove   (C) restore   (D) recover

Unit 25

The Mall of America

If you go to the Minneapolis suburb of Bloomington, Minnesota, you'll find an enormous shopping mall, the Mall of America (MOA). Operating like a small town, the mall employs more than 11,000 people in its more than 520 shops and seven-acre indoor theme park, with 2,000 extras coming to help out over the summer. Also, there are an aquarium complex, Lego Imagination Center, Dinosaur Walk Museum, and a video arcade in the mall.

However, all these names don't really give an idea of just how big the Mall of America really is. For comparison, 32 Boeing 747 airplanes would fit in the **huge** four-story complex. If you spend just 10 minutes in each store, it will take you more than 86 hours to visit them all.

Most people visit the mall to shop at its many high-profile stores, such as Macy's, Bloomingdale's or Nordstrom. Other visitors come to see and experience the mall's seven-acre indoor theme park, with two roller coasters and many exciting rides, games and attractions. It attracts 42 million visitors annually.

If all the shopping and activities make you hungry, there are plenty of places to eat. At least 26 fast food restaurants offer various kinds of food, such as American and Asian foods, or ice cream in many exotic flavors. If you want a more elegant dinner, you could try one of the many sit-down restaurants that feature steaks or seafood.

Despite the cold winters in Minnesota, the mall is kept at a comfortable temperature by sun shining through high windows above the park and by the lighting system. Air conditioning is used year round to keep the air fresh and properly circulating. Whatever the season is, it's always comfortable for visitors to experience one of the world's biggest shopping malls.

_____ 1. How many visitors does the mall draw each year?

(A) 26 million.　　(B) 32 million.　　(C) 42 million.　　(D) 86 million.

_____ 2. The Mall of America is located _____ .

(A) in an area with mild winters

(B) in Bloomington, Minnesota

(C) near the Lego Imagination Center

(D) near Bloomingdale's

_____ 3. Which word in the passage is closest in meaning to "huge"?

(A) Elegant.　　(B) Various.　　(C) Enormous.　　(D) Exotic.

_____ 4. According to the passage, which of the following is NOT true?

(A) There are more than 520 shops in the mall.

(B) Air conditioning systems run all year.

(C) High windows are set up above to let sunlight come through.

(D) The mall has an outdoor theme park with two roller coasters.

_____ 5. Which of the following can be inferred from this passage?

(A) There are more visitors in summer than in the other three seasons.

(B) Most people visit the mall for its theme park.

(C) The mall is the number one tourist attraction in the U.S.

(D) Most visitors come from other countries.

Unit 26

Storm Chasers

In the United States, especially in the flat, open prairie states, tornadoes are very common. During the tornado season, hundreds of unpaid people called recreational storm chasers flock to the tornado states with high-tech equipment that they use to track tornadoes. Some have special vehicles equipped with monitors and detectors, video cameras, strong windows, phones, and roll cages. All these make the vehicles hard to damage if they are caught in a real tornado. Most of these storm chasers follow tornadoes to capture good photographs or video footage.

Although most of these storm chasers prefer to stay some distance away from the expected path of a tornado, others like to get caught in the drama of the storm. These people are thrill-seekers. Using the same expensive equipment as the recreational storm chasers, they stay tuned for up-to-the-minute coverage of tornado positions, which allows them to get as close as possible. They put themselves in great danger, hoping to get the perfect photo or several minutes of video footage to sell to TV networks, calendar publishers and newspapers.

Yet another group of storm chasers lead interested people and work as tour guides. These paid guides follow a tornado at a distance, not risking their lives too greatly, but this still provides people with the thrill of a serious chase. The tour leaders usually have a lot of interesting information to pass on to their customers, while keeping them safe from the tornado's winds, lightning and flying debris.

Many chasers think storm chasing is not very dangerous, but the fact that unpredictable storms **claim** many lives each year cannot be denied. So never try to chase a tornado unless you have received proper safety training.

_____ **1.** How many types of tornado chasers are mentioned in this passage?

    (A) Two.   (B) Three.   (C) Four.   (D) Five

_____ **2.** The up-to-the-minute coverage of tornado positions helps thrill-seekers to

    _____ .

    (A) get as close to tornadoes as possible

    (B) get an idea of how strong a tornado is

    (C) be in great danger

    (D) be reported in local newspapers

_____ **3.** Thrill-seekers _____ .

    (A) want to get recreation by working with good equipment

    (B) want the thrill of being close to tornadoes and want to get paid

    (C) enjoy the thrill of the chase and want to get spectacular photos or videos

    (D) want to sell photos or videos and to offer "chase tour" services

_____ **4.** According to the passage, which of the following is NOT true about the "chase tour" leaders?

    (A) They protect their customers from being harmed by tornadoes.

    (B) They teach their customers a lot about tornadoes.

    (C) They follow tornadoes at a very safe distance.

    (D) They offer tour services for free.

_____ **5.** The word "claim" in the last paragraph can be best replaced by " _____ ."

    (A) risk   (B) give   (C) take   (D) lead

Cyberdating and the Dangers of Internet Romance

Because single men and women are often too busy to meet through traditional dating approaches, many people now look for romance on the Internet. This practice is called cyberdating. One form of cyberdating is talking in Internet chat rooms. If two people **"hit it off"** in a room, they can instant message (IM) each other for a private conversation.

Another form of cyberdating involves personals websites, such as Match.com or Eharmony.com. On these websites, a man or a woman can post a profile with information and a picture. Then, they browse through the profiles of other singles and contact people who interest them via email.

Unfortunately, the Internet is full of "scam artists," people who trick others into giving them money. According to the FBI, over 200,000 Americans lost almost $200 million to Internet scams in 2006 alone. 12% of these scams started in instant messages and 2.4% started in chat rooms. Plus, there are countless stories of people looking for a companion on personals websites only to find **a thief**. Perhaps the worst case is of a woman who gave a man $100,000 to help him with his business only to discover that he was both married and retired.

Those who choose to cyberdate should adopt a few rules to protect themselves. They should avoid answering questions that are too private and be suspicious of anyone who asks for money. Most importantly, if people decide to meet face-to-face, it should always be in a public place.

Cyberdating is a common, modern way of finding romance. For those who are aware of the dangers and take steps to avoid them, it can be both safe and effective.

_____ 1. What's the main idea of this passage?

    (A) Internet users had better watch out for Internet scams.

    (B) Cyberdating is a very safe and effective way to find romance.

    (C) Cyberdating becomes popular, but it carries potential dangers.

    (D) The Internet makes it possible to form relationships with people around the world.

_____ 2. Which of the following is NOT mentioned as an environment the Internet provides for cyberdating?

    (A) Internet chat rooms.   (B) News websites.

    (C) Instant messaging services.   (D) Personals websites.

_____ 3. The phrase "hit it off" in the 1st paragraph probably means _____.

    (A) to like to compete each other   (B) to disagree with others

    (C) to immediately like each other   (D) to meet the same problem

_____ 4. Which of the following is regarded as a "thief" in the 3rd paragraph?

    (A) One who steals identity by using fake websites.

    (B) One who steals financial data through phones and ATMs.

    (C) One who steals banking account and passwords by using false emails.

    (D) One who steals hearts and money by pretending to seek online romance.

_____ 5. Which of the following is NOT mentioned in this passage as a tip for safe cyberdating?

    (A) Always meet in a public place.

    (B) Never give personal information about yourself.

    (C) Be careful if someone asks for financial help.

    (D) Take a friend with you when having the chance to meet in a real life.

A Clean, Green Environmental Scene

"Green building" is the practice of constructing environmentally friendly buildings designed to have a limited impact on the environment. These buildings use less energy for heating, cooling, and lighting than standard buildings, and they are often built on sites surrounded by plants that are native to the area.

The construction of a green building attempts to use materials available nearby. Little or no outside materials are used so that only a few need to be shipped to the site, and as a result, the use of fossil fuels for transportation is kept to a minimum.

One example of a green building is in Rogers, Minnesota. The Rogers High School first minimizes the damage done to the environment by being close to roads that already exist. The design of the buildings allows for natural light to be used efficiently, so that lights are not needed during the daytime. Rather than using air that is pumped in, a vent system is created so that air flows cleanly throughout the buildings without using outside power sources.

Other examples of green buildings are found in Freiburg, Germany. They are homes that are built to use very little power to either heat up in winter or keep cool in summer. People do this by having very good insulation and ventilation systems. The roofs of these houses have solar panels that produce electricity, and they actually produce more electricity than residents need.

For all of us living in the age of global warming, green buildings may be part of the solution to the problem because they lower the amount of waste produced and use clean energy sources. However, they are still not very widespread. To help save our planet, the green building may eventually become the norm in the future.

_____ 1. According to the passage, the main purpose of the use of "green buildings" is to _____ .

(A) lower construction costs (B) reduce environmental impact

(C) improve public health (D) reduce maintenance costs

_____ 2. Which of the following might NOT have been considered by the designer of the Rogers High School?

(A) Construction sites. (B) Reduction of power sources.

(C) Recycled materials. (D) Natural light.

_____ 3. Green buildings in Freiburg, Germany have good insulation and ventilation systems to reduce energy for _____ .

(A) heating and lighting (B) heating and cooling

(C) cooling and drainage (D) cooking and lighting

_____ 4. According to the passage, which of the following is true?

(A) Green buildings do not require greenery.

(B) Green buildings can easily be found everywhere in the world.

(C) Green buildings in Freiburg produce electricity through solar panels.

(D) The Rogers High School uses air conditioning systems to pump fresh air into its buildings.

_____ 5. The purpose of using as many local building materials as possible in the construction of green buildings is to _____ .

(A) help local businesses prosper

(B) set a new standard for the future

(C) minimize the need for extra materials

(D) reduce the amount of energy used for transportation

Homeschooling or Traditional Education?

These days, homeschooling is on the rise. More and more parents choose to provide education for their children in their own home.

Why do these parents choose homeschooling? Some believe that children in public schools experience too much peer pressure, making it harder for them to develop good character traits. Other parents are dissatisfied with the instructional programs of standard schools. They want to decide what is important for their children to learn, rather than leaving it to the government bureaucracy. Besides, home schools allow children to work at a level that is appropriate to their own developmental stage. Skills and concepts can be introduced at the right time.

Teaching methods at homeschools vary. Some parents follow a strict schedule and imitate a traditional school environment. Other parents follow **a radical form of homeschooling** in which they do not give grades or tests and allow their children to study whatever they want. Most parents, however, follow the middle path to provide a balance between freedom and structure.

Recent studies in the United States have shown that homeschooled children score just as high on the SAT as regular students. Also, because colleges look for students with unique experiences, homeschooled students are slightly more successful in college admissions. Homeschooled students tend to do better in subjects like English and art, but they are slightly less skilled at math and science.

There are many trade-offs to consider when parents decide whether or not to homeschool their children. Homeschooling can be expensive, and at least one parent must be home full-time to supervise the education. In addition, many homeschooled students are lonely. They may want to belong to school teams. Homeschooling also requires a lot of discipline from both the parents and the children. However, it is generally believed that the benefits of homeschooling far outweigh its drawbacks.

_____ 1. What is the author's attitude toward homeschooling?
　　(A) For it.　　　　(B) Against it.　　(C) Neutral.　　　　(D) Doubtful.

_____ 2. Which of the following is not mentioned as a factor resulting in the increasing number of homeschooled students?
　　(A) Peer pressure.　　　　　　　　(B) Educational achievement.
　　(C) Safety concerns.　　　　　　　(D) Educational programs.

_____ 3. Which of the following is NOT true about homeschooling?
　　(A) Homeschooled children score as well as regular students on the SAT.
　　(B) Being accepted by colleges could be easier for homeschooled students.
　　(C) Homeschooled children might be socially isolated.
　　(D) Homeschooled students score a lot higher in math and science.

_____ 4. In the 3rd paragraph, "a radical form of homeschooling" provides children with a lot of _____ .
　　(A) structure　　　(B) freedom　　　(C) service　　　(D) planning

_____ 5. It can be inferred from the passage that _____ .
　　(A) parents who homeschool children are generally more knowledgeable
　　(B) only parents can decide whether homschooling is right for their family
　　(C) both parents and children may lose self-control during the homeschooling process
　　(D) homeschooled students are smart, mature, creative and independent

Unit 30

The ORBIS Story

In the mid-1970s, Dr. David Paton, a Houston-based ophthalmologist, was troubled by what he saw as curable eye diseases going untreated in the developing world. He came up with a plan to put technology and skills into an airplane and create a "flying eye hospital" that could go wherever **it** was needed. In addition to providing care for patients in developing countries, Dr. Paton's intention was to help educate local doctors so that they could carry on the practice.

In 1982, with a grant from the US Agency for International Development and some private donations, ORBIS International was founded. A retired DC-8 airplane was donated by United Airlines to become the first "flying eye hospital." After being **converted** into a fully functional teaching eye hospital, it was put into service. In 1982 it flew to Panama on its first training mission. Since then, ORBIS has been striving to eliminate unnecessary blindness and restore eyesight in developing nations.

Today, ORBIS has become a well-known international non-profit and non-governmental organization that offers free medical treatment and training for the prevention of blindness. All ORBIS members are volunteers, including more than 400 medical professionals and 17 pilots for the "flying eye hospital," which is now a DC-10, bought by ORBIS in 1992 for $14 million. Its first operational mission was to Beijing, China in 1994. The new aircraft is equipped with an operating room, a recovery room and a classroom.

ORBIS also runs hospital-based programs in several countries, and works with local medical organizations on blindness prevention and treatment for eye diseases. It is estimated that more than one million people have been treated by ORBIS, and over 124,000 local healthcare professionals from more than 80 countries have enhanced their skills through ORBIS programs.

_____ 1. ORBIS International's mission is to _____.

    (A) establish permanent government programs for eye doctors

    (B) operate hospital-based programs in developed countries

    (C) treat eye diseases and educate local doctors in developing countries

    (D) provide education and training for eye doctors around the world

_____ 2. The current "flying eye hospital" _____.

    (A) is a DC-8 donated by United Airlines

    (B) was placed into service in 1992

    (C) is a DC-10 aircraft bought by ORBIS in 1994

    (D) contains an operating room, a recovery room, and a classroom

_____ 3. The pronoun "it" in the 1st paragraph refers to _____.

    (A) technology   (B) ophthalmologist

    (C) flying eye hospital   (D) plan

_____ 4. The word "converted" in the 2nd paragraph can best replaced by "_____."

    (A) transformed   (B) transported

    (C) dismissed   (D) delivered

_____ 5. According to the passage, which of the following is true?

    (A) ORBIS International was established in 1992.

    (B) The idea for ORBIS came from Dr. David Paton in the 1970s.

    (C) The first training mission of the "flying eye hospital " was to China.

    (D) The pilots for the mobile hospital are not volunteers.

Unit 31

The Monster of Loch Ness

Up in the Scottish Highlands is a beautiful lake called Loch Ness. The lake is famous for its resident, the monster "Nessie."

Evidence of a strange water creature was first noted some 1500 years ago in the biography of a saint. However, it did not make the headlines until 1930, when three fishermen reported seeing a disturbance in the water where a giant dragon-like animal about 20 feet long suddenly appeared. Though their boat rocked violently, the monster did not do them any harm. Following the story, many people claimed to have seen a strange figure, which was called "Nessie" after the lake. The monster was not known to cause any harm; people even considered the sighting to be a good omen.

No one knows for sure what it looks like. Some say it resembles a long-neck alligator without claws. Others have described a giant snake-like animal with a red mouth and huge horns sticking out.

A Scottish engineer named Robert Craig has come up with the best possible explanation, published in 1982. He claims that the so-called monster is in reality the **submerged** trunks of Scots pine trees that surround the area. Having been submerged for years at the bottom of the loch, they sometime rise to the surface because of a difference in pressure. As they do so, the gas inside the trunks is released, causing ripples and bubbles in the water. Then the trunks sink again, probably for the last time.

Some believe that there is no such thing as a monster and that Nessie is only a myth. Yet the majority of people refuse to believe the theory and they continue to gather around the lake to have a glimpse of their dear Nessie.

_____ 1. The monster got its name "Nessie" from _____.

    (A) the man who first reported it

    (B) the lake it lives in

    (C) the man who first took a photo of it

    (D) the shape of the lake it lives in

_____ 2. When did the first recorded sighting of the monster appear?

    (A) In 1939.   (B) In 1982.

    (C) In the 6th century.   (D) In the 16th century.

_____ 3. Which of the flowing is NOT true about the 1930 report of sighting?

    (A) The monster was thought to be about 20 feet in length.

    (B) The monster was thought to be a large fish-like animal.

    (C) The sighting attracted public attention.

    (D) The monster didn't cause any injury to the three fishermen.

_____ 4. The word "submerged" in the 4th paragraph is closest in meaning to "_____."

    (A) floating   (B) emerging

    (C) developed   (D) underwater

_____ 5. According to Robert Craig's theory, which of the following is true?

    (A) The so-called monster is simply oak tree trunks.

    (B) The monster rises to the surface to breathe.

    (C) The monster looks like an alligator.

    (D) Pressure differences result in the appearance of the so-called monster.

Unit 32

The First Postage Stamp

Before 1840, stamps did not exist in Britain. Postage was either written or marked with ink on the envelope. The receiver, rather than the sender, had to pay for the delivery costs. Postmen had a great task of collecting postage from reluctant receivers when they delivered the mail. Sometimes, people refused to accept letters because the postal rates were too high. They could not afford to use the mail system.

In 1837, Rowland Hill proposed his revolutionary idea of a uniform low rate of one penny to send a letter anywhere in Britain in *Post Office Reform: Its Importance and Practicability*. He also suggested that the sender, not the addressee, should pay for the postage, that the basis for payment should be changed from distance to weight, and that postage should be pre-paid by placing a specially designed label on the outside of envelopes. His proposal was heavily debated for several years. After serious discussion, Rowland Hill's proposal was finally adopted. On May 6, 1840, the world's first postage stamp was born in Britain. It cost one penny and bore the profile of Queen Victoria's head.

The stamp became known as the Penny Black, because it was printed in black. The Penny Black had a dramatic effect. It changed the world of communication, just as email has done today. After the introduction of the Penny Black, millions of letters were written and sent each year because almost everybody could afford it. This system of sending mail was such a good idea that it spread very fast around the world. It didn't take long for other countries to copy the system. In 1843, Brazil was the second country in the world to use an adhesive postage stamp, known as "Bull's Eye," and in 1847, the U.S Government officially issued its first stamps, bearing portraits of Benjamin Franklin. By 1860, over 90 countries and colonies were issuing postage stamps.

_____ 1. The first country to issue postage stamps was _____.

    (A) the United States   (B) Britain

    (C) Germany   (D) Brazil

_____ 2. What did the world's first postage stamp look like?

    (A) It was a black stamp with a picture of Queen Victoria's head on it.

    (B) It was a black-and-white stamp with Benjamin Franklin on it

    (C) It was a blue stamp bearing a picture of a bull's eye.

    (D) It was a red stamp with a picture of Queen Elizabeth's head.

_____ 3. Which of the following is NOT true about the postal system before 1840?

    (A) The cost of mailing a letter was very high.

    (B) The postage depended on the distance.

    (C) Postmen had to expend much effort collecting money from senders.

    (D) Receivers had to pay for the postage.

_____ 4. Which word in the passage is a synonym of the word "receiver"?

    (A) Reform.   (B) Profile.

    (C) Sender.   (D) Addressee.

_____ 5. It can be inferred that _____.

    (A) the Penny Black was also available in Britain's colonies

    (B) the first American postage stamp was designed by Benjamin Franklin

    (C) before 1840 the postal service in Britain led to a lot of public dissatisfaction and criticism

    (D) Britain is the only country that always has the head of a queen on its stamps

Man's Best Friend Learns a New Trick

Recent studies have shown that a dog's olfactory senses may be even better than we initially thought. Researchers claim that dogs possess the ability to smell cancer. In 1989, an article in the *Lancet* medical journal reported that a dog kept smelling a mole on his owner's leg, which turned out to be skin cancer.

Then in 2004, the *British Medical Journal* published a study on dogs managing to pick out smells for bladder cancer. Dr. Carolyn Willis and her team trained six dogs of various breeds and ages over seven months to distinguish between urine from patients with bladder cancer and urine from patients without bladder cancer. Overall, the dogs correctly selected the bladder caner urine on 22 out of 54 occasions.

In 2006, a new study conducted by the Pine Street Foundation in California reported that ordinary household dogs, with only a few weeks of basic training, learned to accurately distinguish between breath samples of lung and breast cancer patients and healthy subjects. Michael Broffman and Michael McCulloch said the success rate was 88 percent with the breast cancer samples and 99 percent with the lung cancer ones.

A dog's nose is a finely tuned instrument, capable of distinguishing smells one thousand times weaker than those a human nose can detect. Cancer cells release organic substances as they grow. A dog's olfactory power is strong enough to sense and distinguish **them** even though the amounts are very tiny.

Since dogs really can detect cancer, what does the future hold? Some researchers think that dogs will be used in doctors' offices as "early warning systems" for detecting cancer in patients. Other researchers hope to use Fido's nose as the blueprint for a new "mechanical nose," one that would work like the dog's nose but without the need for frequent walks.

_____ **1.** Olfactory senses are senses of _____ .

(A) taste   (B) smell   (C) hearing   (D) sight

_____ **2.** Which of the following is true about Dr. Willis' study?

(A) The study was published in an American medical journal in 2004.

(B) Six dogs of the same breed were taught to sniff out the urine from patients with bladder cancer.

(C) She indicated that dogs could detect characteristics of skin cancer.

(D) The percentage of success of the dogs in Dr. Willis's experiment was about 41%.

_____ **3.** The purpose of Broffman and McCulloch's study was to find out if

_____ .

(A) cancer could be smelled on a person's breath

(B) dogs could smell a tumor on the skin

(C) dogs of different breeds had different olfactory abilities

(D) the dog's nose is one thousand times more sensitive than the human nose

_____ **4.** The pronoun "them" in the 4th paragraph refers to _____ .

(A) cells   (B) amounts   (C) substances   (D) smells

_____ **5.** It can be inferred that _____ .

(A) it would not be practical to use dogs to detect cancer

(B) scientists ultimately hope to develop new devices that rival Fido's nose to detect cancer cells

(C) dogs will be able to sniff out the smell of cancer in blood

(D) dogs will be able to help humans by identifying the stage of lung cancer

Unit 34

Think Pink

Did you know that the Pink Panther character was created for a movie but wasn't actually in the film? The movie was made in 1963 and was called *The Pink Panther*. It involved the theft of a valuable diamond, followed by the funny adventures of a clumsy French detective who tried to solve the crime. The "Pink Panther" in the movie was the name of the diamond, and it had a flaw inside. When looked at closely, the flaw resembled a pink panther.

The makers of the movie needed something for its opening title and closing credits, so they decided to make a short cartoon. Naturally, they chose a pink cartoon panther. The movie was very successful, and many sequels were made. The Pink Panther character was a hit with the public. Not only was he used again in the other movies, but short movies and a long-running cartoon series on TV featuring the character were also made. Interestingly, the cartoons have international appeal because there is no talking. **This** makes it quite easy to understand as the audience only have to watch what happens while the equally famous Pink Panther theme music plays in the background.

The Pink Panther was very popular in the late 60s and into the 70s. The creators had the character licensed, and the Pink Panther began to appear as toys and on all kinds of merchandise. He was also used in advertising and was a favorite of any company that wanted to sell something pink. In fact, he was the spokesperson of Owens Corning fiberglass insulation, which came up with the memorable slogan, "Think Pink!"

Although he's never really disappeared, the Pink Panther received more attention in 2006 with a remake of the original movie. It will be quite a long time before he is forgotten. Don't think so? Just ask someone what they think of when they think "pink."

_____ 1. The diamond was named the "Pink Panther" because _____.

    (A) it was its owner's name

    (B) it was the title of the movie

    (C) the flaw inside looked like a pink panther

    (D) it was the hottest cartoon character

_____ 2. What is the original movie mainly about?

    (A) The quality of a diamond.   (B) The theft of a diamond.

    (C) An adventurous vacation.   (D) The clumsiness of the Pink Panther.

_____ 3. Which of the following is NOT true about the Pink Panther character?

    (A) Toys with the character on them appeared under license in the 70s.

    (B) It originally appeared in the opening and the end of the 1963 movie.

    (C) It did not become popular until the 70s.

    (D) Its popularity brought about cartoon series on TV.

_____ 4. The pronoun "this" in the 2nd paragraph refers to "_____."

    (A) featuring the character   (B) theme music

    (C) international appeal   (D) no talking

_____ 5. It can be inferred that _____.

    (A) the color pink is a trademark for Owens Corning fiberglass insulation

    (B) the new movie, *The Pink Panther*, became a hit in 2006

    (C) the Pink Panther will not be remembered for a long time

    (D) several Pink Panther films have been made, only two of which have "Pink Panther" in the title

Book Summaries

Kesey, Ken. *One Flew Over the Cuckoo's Nest*. Pan Books, Ltd., 1962. 255 pages.

> The orderly lives of some mental institution patients are greatly changed by the appearance of a loud and energetic patient named R.P. McMurphy. After his arrival, we see McMurphy "fight the system" by disobeying the orders of the Big Nurse. McMurphy works to turn his fellow patients against the Big Nurse, who fights back by lying to the patients and using her authority to control them. This results in some deaths and in the freedom of body and mind for some patients.

Garcia Marquez, Gabriel. *One Hundred Years of Solitude*. Harper&Row, 1970. 383 pages.

> Taking place in the fictional town of Macondo, *One Hundred Years of Solitude* tells the story of the Buendia family. Over seven generations, Macondo and the Buendia family suffer wars, invasions and floods. Much of the story involves magical realism, a writing style in which seemingly impossible things happen—such as animals talking and people flying—in a very realistic setting.

Dickey, James. *Deliverance*. Dell Publishing, 1970. 278 pages.

> Four men decide to take a small boat down the fictional Cahulawassee, Georgia's largest and most remote river. While their trip starts out quietly, things quickly turn dangerous as the men must fight against an unexpectedly wild and raging river, as well as dangerous people who live in the woods. This book was named one of the 100 most important novels of the 20th century.

Hornby, Nick. *About a Boy*. Indigo, 1998. 286 pages.

> This story relates the friendship of a lonely, bullied schoolboy named

Marcus and a rich, bored 36-year-old man named Will. The boy's mother is very odd and doesn't understand that he needs to fit in with the other kids at school. Will has no ambition in life and lives off the money his father made. The story was made into a movie of the same name in 2002.

_____ 1. Which book is the thickest?
    (A) *One Flew Over the Cuckoo's Nest.*   (B) *One Hundred Years of Solitude.*
    (C) *Deliverance.*   (D) *About a Boy.*

_____ 2. Which book was made into a film in 2002?
    (A) *One Flew Over the Cuckoo's Nest.*   (B) *One Hundred Years of Solitude.*
    (C) *Deliverance.*   (D) *About a Boy.*

_____ 3. Which book talks about the seven generations of a family?
    (A) *One Flew Over the Cuckoo's Nest.*   (B) *One Hundred Years of Solitude.*
    (C) *Deliverance.*   (D) *About a Boy.*

_____ 4. Who wrote the book about four men's adventurous trip down a river?
    (A) Ken Kesey.   (B) Gabriel Garcia Marquez.
    (C) James Dickey.   (D) Nick Hornby.

_____ 5. Who wrote the book that describes what happens in a mental institution?
    (A) Ken Kesey.   (B) Gabriel Garcia Marquez.
    (C) James Dickey.   (D) Nick Hornby.

Unit 36

The Spirit of Singing

Several features of Negro spirituals have influenced the development of American music. Negro spirituals arose in the early 19th century from the music of American slaves, who were often forced to convert to Christianity. They combined the hope of their new faith with traditional African songs to create unique American musical styles.

One feature of Negro spirituals was the "shout." People repeatedly **chanted** a line while dancing quickly in a circle, a tradition that came from African religions. After the 1930s, spirituals became known as "gospel music," but parts of the "shout" remained in many songs.

A second feature of Negro spirituals was the "call and response," in which a leader sang a line and the singers answered with the next line. Ray Charles, the blind American singer famous for mixing musical styles, used this technique in non-spiritual songs such as "What I'd Say" and "Hit the Road Jack." Although some members of the black Christian community criticized Charles for using the "call and response," it became a popular feature in early rock and roll music, which featured strong singing and a quick tempo.

An important modern musical style with spiritual influences is rhythm and blues, or "R&B." This kind of music has had a huge impact in America. Combining gospel singing with jazz instruments and blues beats, R&B sounds can be heard in rock and roll artists such as Elvis Presley and the Rolling Stones, as well as modern hip hop artists like Mary J. Blige and Justin Timberlake.

Although Negro spirituals began as a source of comfort for the slaves, they have grown into a major source of inspiration for generations of American musicians. Their influence helped create unique American music that is recognized around the world.

_____ 1. The main purpose of this passage is to explain _____.

(A) the features of rhythm and blues

(B) the development and the influence of Negro spirituals

(C) the difference between rock and roll and R&B

(D) Negro spirituals' influence on music around the world

_____ 2. According to the passage, which of the following is true?

(A) Negro spirituals date back to the late 19th century.

(B) Negro spirituals were born when American slaves were released.

(C) Negro spirituals used the "call and response" between a leader and singers.

(D) "Gospel music" had a great influence on the development of Negro spirituals.

_____ 3. The word "chanted" in the 2nd paragraph can be best replaced by "_____."

(A) painted   (B) drew   (C) sang   (D) kept

_____ 4. It can be inferred from this passage that the slaves created spirituals to _____.

(A) relieve their sufferings   (B) entertain their owners

(C) show their high spirits   (D) express thanks to their owners

_____ 5. Which of the following is NOT a factor that contributed to the development of Negro spirituals?

(A) The condition of slavery.   (B) African traditions.

(C) Faith in God.   (D) American Indian traditions.

Fat-free, Fur-free?

In today's fashion industry, two major issues are currently making headlines around the world. One affects the lives of humans while the other affects those of animals.

From the 1960s onwards, fashion increasingly demanded that models should be extremely thin. This belief that "skinny means success" has left many models struggling with eating disorders. Critics also believe that many vulnerable teenage girls study photos of thin models, and then attempt to look the same. This, they say, has contributed to a growing rate of eating diseases, like anorexia and bulimia, among young girls.

Recently, a slight change has finally been seen in the fashion industry. In 2006, Madrid Fashion Week banned all extremely thin models from its catwalks. Organizers said they did this to try to promote a healthier image for young girls. However, most designers still prefer the thinnest models, even though a supermodel, Luisel Ramos, recently died from anorexia.

The second important issue facing the fashion industry is the use of animal fur in clothes. The anti-fur charity "InFURmation" says that more than fifty million animals are killed every year for their fur, and that some of the most popular choices are foxes, rabbits and wolves. Some top fashion designers like Calvin Klein and Jay McCarroll, have banned the use of fur in their collections. Sadly, 2006 and 2007 have seen a new interest in the use of fur, and fur clothing has reappeared in fashion stores.

Some people argue that people should be able to make their own choices about their weight and the material their clothes are made from. Nevertheless, the fashion industry, with its power to influence public opinion, should certainly be responsible for promoting good principles. If models of a sensible weight wore only non-fur products, the world would surely be full of healthier, happier young women, as well as healthier, happier animals.

_____ 1. The passage is mainly about _____ .
　　　　(A) super-thin models and eating diseases
　　　　(B) eating diseases and fashion designers
　　　　(C) super-thin models and the use of fur
　　　　(D) fashion designers and the use of fur

_____ 2. Madrid Fashion Week banned super-thin models to _____ .
　　　　(A) make headlines　　　　　　　(B) set a new fashion trend
　　　　(C) project a healthier body image　　(D) promote fashion products

_____ 3. "InFURmation" might be an organization working to _____ .
　　　　(A) ban super-thin models from catwalks
　　　　(B) stop people from killing animals for their fur
　　　　(C) help teenage girls who suffer from anorexia
　　　　(D) protect wild animals, such as foxes and wolves

_____ 4. According to the passage, which of the following is NOT true?
　　　　(A) Since the 1960s, people have always liked skinny models.
　　　　(B) Super-thin catwalk models have a negative impact on teenage girls.
　　　　(C) Calvin Klein no longer uses fur in its collections.
　　　　(D) Most designers are following Madrid's lead to ban extremely thin models.

_____ 5. What is the author's attitude towards the two bans?
　　　　(A) For them.　　　　　　　　　(B) Against them.
　　　　(C) Neutral.　　　　　　　　　　(D) Indifferent.

The Truth About Vitamins

Modern science allows people to get all of the vitamins that they need from a pill. People in the United States spend $23 billion on synthetic vitamins every year. However, are these synthetic nutrients as healthy as natural vitamins that come from food?

A major concern with synthetic vitamins is that many countries do not closely **regulate** them. For example, the United States government asks companies that make synthetic vitamins to list the ingredients on bottle labels, but it does not test these claims or punish those who break the rules. **Companies may also lie about the ingredients in their vitamins.** For example, some vitamins have been found to contain too much lead, which could result in serious illnesses. In addition, some synthetic vitamins do not actually contain the amounts of nutrients **they** claim to provide. This means that people who take these pills are not getting as many vitamins as they think.

In contrast, real food provides people with plenty of natural vitamins without the risks that come with synthetic pills. If people eat a well-balanced diet that includes many fruits and vegetables, they will receive all of the vitamins that they need to live well. People should try to eat only natural foods and avoid artificial food products as much as possible. It is also important that people eat a wide variety of foods. This will make certain that they receive many types of vitamins from many different sources.

Even though synthetic vitamins are convenient, people must not rely on them for their dietary requirements. Instead, people can get their vitamins from natural food, which is the best way to live a long, healthy life.

_____ 1. What is the author's attitude to synthetic vitamins?

    (A) Positive.   (B) Negative.

    (C) Neutral.   (D) Indifferent.

_____ 2. The word "regulate" in the 2nd paragraph means to _____.

    (A) encourage by a prize

    (B) manage in a normal way

    (C) control by means of laws or rules

    (D) arrange in a strict way

_____ 3. What's the author's purpose of mentioning "Companies may also lie about the ingredients in their vitamins"?

    (A) To explain how these companies make profits.

    (B) To explain why synthetic vitamins are useless in our bodies.

    (C) To compare the amounts of ingredients produced and claimed.

    (D) To discuss the risks we face when consuming synthetic vitamins.

_____ 4. According to the passage, which of the following is NOT true?

    (A) Natural vitamins are derived from real food.

    (B) Some synthetic vitamins have been found to contain harmful minerals.

    (C) A well-balanced diet provides us with all the natural vitamins we need.

    (D) In the U.S., millions of dollars are spent on synthetic vitamins per year.

_____ 5. The pronoun "they" in the 2nd paragraph refers to _____.

    (A) ingredients

    (B) people

    (C) some synthetic vitamins

    (D) nutrients

Unit 39

Shopaholics

Shopaholics are people who are addicted to shopping. Most of them are experiencing frustration or depression in their daily lives. For them, shopping is a temporary escape from these negative feelings. A recent study conducted by Dr. Koran shows that about six percent of the U.S. population falls into this group—outnumbering the country's gambling addicts, and men and women suffer equally.

Some social conditions are also responsible for the shopaholic phenomenon. The easy availability of credit cards encourages people to buy now and worry about financial responsibility later. The Internet and TV shopping channels also make shopping even easier. Pop culture is another factor. With magazines or books like the *Shopaholic* series and TV shows like *Sex and the City*, shopping has become a need in our lives.

Shopping has become an extra problem for all these people. They can be so preoccupied with shopping that they don't have enough time to spend with their friends or family members. This can destroy their relationships. What's more, their excessive use of credit cards often leads to overwhelming debt. The anxiety caused by their huge debts may result in deeper depression.

Psychologists suggest that they face the facts. Shopholics should admit that their reckless shopping trips mean disorder in their lives. Having realized this, they can start to **confront**, rather than run away from, what's really bothering them. Some American psychologists have created addiction recovery programs. Shopaholics are taught how to control their shopping habits. For example, they are told to cancel their credit cards and shop only with cash. They are also encouraged to do other activities when they suddenly feel the need to go shopping.

_____ 1. Which of the following is NOT mentioned as a factor that leads to shopping addictions?

(A) Psychological factors.　　　　　　(B) Social factors.

(C) Cultural factors.　　　　　　　　(D) Biological factors.

_____ 2. Which of the following is NOT mentioned as a problem caused by shopping addictions?

(A) Financial problems.　　　　　　　(B) Occupational problems.

(C) Psychological problems.　　　　　(D) Interpersonal problems.

_____ 3. The word "confront" in the 4th paragraph can be best replaced by

_____ .

(A) trap　　　　(B) escape　　　　(C) face　　　　(D) deceive

_____ 4. Addiction recovery programs are created to _____ .

(A) use drugs as a treatment for shopaholics

(B) provide shopaholics with behavior therapy

(C) teach shopaholics how to control drug addictions

(D) help shopaholics learn how to shop with credit cards

_____ 5. According to the passage, which of the following is NOT true?

(A) Some shopaholics are using shopping as a solution to depression.

(B) Shopping is made easier because of the Internet and TV shopping programs.

(C) Men are just as likely to suffer from shopping addiction as women.

(D) In the U.S., gambling addicts are more than shopaholics.

Unit 40

Big Apple Bans Trans Fats

NEW YORK, Dec. 5 — The New York City Board of Health unanimously approved the world's first ban on the use of almost all trans fats in restaurants.

Health Commissioner Dr. Thomas R. Frieden claimed that the ban was an answer to citizens who wanted harmful trans fats removed from restaurant food. Businesses will have 18 months to replace trans fats with healthier options. After then, food items must contain less than 0.5 grams of trans fats per serving.

Trans fats were invented in the early 20th century. Made by adding hydrogen to vegetable oil, trans fats became popular with food producers in the 1970s as a replacement for harmful saturated fats. Restaurant owners prefer trans fats because they have a long shelf life and make food crispier.

The city government says that removing trans fats from restaurant food will save lives. Artificial trans fats raise bad cholesterol and lower good cholesterol in the blood stream. Medical studies have found that consuming trans fats increases the risks of heart disease, stroke, and premature death.

Health professionals and citizens supported the ban, and medical groups voiced complete support. Mayor Michael R. Bloomberg also defended the decision. "Nobody wants to take away your French fries and hamburgers," said Bloomberg, but he stressed that they should be made healthier.

However, business groups opposed the ban. Dan Fleischer, a spokesman for the National Restaurant Association, called it a "misguided attempt" to legislate health. Restaurant owners also expressed concern. They said the ban would be difficult for their businesses but were grateful to have 18 months to search for other ways to cook their food.

_____ 1. Consuming trans fats increases the risk of heart disease by _____.

    (A) raising bad cholesterol and lowering good cholesterol

    (B) affecting people's mood very negatively

    (C) lowering nutrient levels in the food people eat

    (D) raising people's stress levels and affecting blood sugar

_____ 2. According to the passage, restaurants use trans fats for its _____.

    (A) flavor and low price   (B) storage life and taste difference

    (C) rich nutrients and flavor   (D) low price and convenience

_____ 3. According to the passage, which of the following is NOT true?

    (A) Most New York citizens supported the ban.

    (B) The Board of Health allowed 18 months for businesses to replace trans fats.

    (C) Trans fats are created when hydrogen is added to animal fats.

    (D) Trans fats didn't gain popularity among food companies until the 1970s.

_____ 4. Which of the following might be what Dr. Frieden would say?

    (A) "Mayor Bloomberg just wants to grab headlines."

    (B) "Trans fats do not affect heart health in such a negative way."

    (C) "No one will miss trans fats when they are removed."

    (D) "New York City has no right to legislate health."

_____ 5. It can be inferred from this passage that _____.

    (A) the prices of fast food in New York will go up

    (B) New Yorkers will eat more French fries and hamburgers

    (C) other cities will follow New York City and approve the same ban

    (D) food companies are finding or developing new oils to replace trans fats

Note

Answer Key

01. DDACA	21. BCABC
02. CBABD	22. BDADC
03. ADDBC	23. DCBBA
04. CBDBC	24. CDCAB
05. ACDBA	25. CBCDA
06. ACADB	26. BACDC
07. BCADD	27. CBCDD
08. BACAB	28. BCBCD
09. BDCAD	29. ACDBC
10. CBBDC	30. CDCAB
11. ABBAC	31. BCBDD
12. DACDA	32. BACDC
13. CDDAA	33. BDACB
14. CBCBD	34. CBCDA
15. ACBDC	35. BDBCA
16. CCBAD	36. BCCAD
17. DABCD	37. CCBDA
18. CDBBC	38. BCDDC
19. BDCBD	39. DBCBD
20. CDBAC	40. ABCCD

字彙翻譯HOW EASY

王隆興　編著

大考字彙與翻譯　一次搞定 HOW EASY！

1. 彙集歷屆大考精選單字500個，撰寫成情境豐富的文意字彙題利用這些測驗，保證讓您不僅能記下單字，更能達到活用 HOW EASY！
2. 綜合多元且生活化的各類翻譯題目，讓您輕鬆做好翻譯練習、徹底厚植翻譯實力，保證面對大考翻譯感覺 HOW EASY！
3. 解析本收錄字彙題幹完整中譯、重點單字片語整理；翻譯部分則有重點句型及文法歸納，善用本書的豐富內容，保證讓您英文進步 HOW EASY！

From Cloze Test to Translation Practice
從克漏字到翻譯練習

王郁惠 鄭翔嬬　編著

誰說克漏字與翻譯不能一次解決？

1. 克漏字測驗主題多達20種主題共30個單元，每個單元皆有兩篇短篇及一篇長篇測驗，讓您充分熟悉各式主題，幫助您同時兼顧字句用法及段落主旨。
2. 連貫式翻譯每回提供3組練習題目，2個重要句型講解、每個題組中所需的關鍵字彙，透過反覆練習，提昇您翻譯寫作能力。
3. 隨書附有解析本，提供詳實文章的全文翻譯，幫助您確實掌握文章細節脈絡，並學習相關解題技巧及應答策略。

Basic English Grammar Guide
英文文法入門指引

呂香瑩 著

以國中英語課程為基準，以高中或高職一、二年級必學的基礎文法為目標，將文法觀念化繁為簡，屏除讀者對文法學習的惶恐之心，進而了解、活用文法。

1. 十三個精心整理的章節，讓您迅速掌握文法重點、提升英文程度。
   實用的內容、重點式的解析和即時演練，幫您破解文法上的難題。
2. 特別規劃『學習小秘訣』單元，協助您一眼就記住文法關鍵。

A Practical Guide to English Grammar
英文文法快速攻略

周 彥 編著

1. 統整國、高中必備的基礎英文文法，讓您溫故知新，同時循序漸進地加強英文實力。
2. 以淺顯易懂的例句、簡單明瞭的圖表說明，讓您擺脫繁瑣的文法規則，重新學習英文文法。
3. 『停看聽』及實用演練習題單元讓您有效地奠定文法基礎，融會貫通重要概念。

Reading Power 系列

Intermediate

★ 中級全民英檢必備
★ 學科能力測驗／指定科目考試／統一入學測驗必備

Intermediate Reading ②
完全閱讀導引

翻譯與解析

李文玲　編著

三民書局

01 冰人詛咒
The Curse of the Iceman

　　1991 年夏末，德籍旅人赫爾穆特・賽門 (Helmut Simon) 在奧地利登山。他突然發現身穿皮衣的冷凍屍體躺在冰地上。賽門對外宣布他的發現，認為他找到幾百年前在寒天喪命的獵人。後來專業登山家科特・弗里茨 (Kurt Fritz) 帶著一群由瑞能・亨因博士 (Rainer Henn) 所率領的科學家抵達當地。幾週後，冰屍移轉至科學實驗室的過程便以紀錄片的方式在世界各地播放。

　　接著，曾經接觸過這具史前冰屍的人開始一一罹難。首先，1992 年，瑞能・亨因博士在開車去發表有關冰人的演講途中車禍身亡。接著，登山家科特・弗里茨在登山時也遇到雪崩罹難。接連發生兩起意外事件後，媒體開始對「冰人」帶來的厄運議論紛紛。當瑞能・霍澤爾 (Rainer Hoelzl) 拍完關於冰屍電視專輯數月後也離奇病死時，冰人詛咒之說便開始廣為流傳。

　　冰人發現者赫爾穆特・賽門認為這些傳言都是無稽之談。當他獲判有權因「冰屍觀光客」而獲得金錢後，決定重登舊地慶祝一番。他卻突遇暴風雪，而失足跌入二百米懸崖喪生。後來，新的研究團隊隊長孔納德・施平德勒 (Konrad Spindler) 在公開表明這些死亡只不過是不幸意外後，幾週後也跟著過世。最後，2005 年，湯姆・洛伊 (Tom Loy) 博士在完成冰人相關著作以前也死亡了。

1. 本文主旨為何？
　(A) 人們普遍認為冰人的死亡詛咒是荒謬之論。
　(B) 儘管有些科學家很努力，許多關於冰人的生與死的問題仍是無解之謎。
　(C) 數百位科學家介入研究這個保存良好的木乃伊。
　(D) 謠傳和冰人有接觸的人會因詛咒而死。
　本文主要在談關於冰人的詛咒，許多人的死因似乎和冰人有關。

2. 依據本文，多少人因為和冰人有接觸而死亡？
　(A) 3 人　(B) 4 人　(C) 5 人　**(D) 6 人**
　見第二、三段。

3. 冰人被發現 ＿＿＿＿＿ 。
　(A) 穿著皮衣
　(B) 在幾百年前
　(C) (被)登山客科特・弗里茨(發現)
　(D) (被)德國人類學家(發現)
　見第一段第二句。

4. 依據本文，以下何者為真？
　(A) 詛咒的謠言在 1992 年隨著瑞能・霍澤爾的死亡而開始。
　(B) 電影製作人瑞能・亨因死於神秘疾病。
　(C) 赫爾穆特・賽門死於意外的暴風雪。
　(D) 團隊領導人科特・弗里茨在去發表有關冰人的演講途中死於車禍。
　第二、三段介紹死者和死因。

5. 以下何者可能是孔納德・施平德勒過世前數週公開說的話？
　(A)「這詛咒根本是媒體虛構的。」
　(B)「死亡詛咒會繼續謠傳。」
　(C)「這個木乃伊被詛咒了。」
　(D)「詛咒恐怕是真的。」
　見第三段第四句。

curse	n.; v.	詛咒	preserve	v.	保存
transfer	n.	移轉	documentary film		紀錄片
media	n. (pl.)	媒體	spread	v.	流傳

mummy　n.　木乃伊
prehistoric　adj.　史前的
ridiculous　adj.　荒謬的

據信早在西元 500 年，曾經統治墨西哥與南美部分地區的馬雅人便率先發現巧克力。可可樹原產於當地，而巧克力是由可可籽所製造的。馬雅人發現，以粉狀可可籽沖泡的飲料可以增長肌肉與提神。

幾百年後，阿茲特克人掌權時，巧克力更受歡迎。阿茲特克人認為巧克力有療效，只保留給王公貴族與戰士食用。

歐洲人一直到 16 世紀中葉才知道巧克力的存在。哥倫布多次航向美洲的旅程中，某次看到當地人虔誠地捧著狀似核果的豆子，他誤以為那是小杏仁。不過，直到另一位西班牙探險家赫南多・科爾特斯 (Hernando Cortez) 幾年後航行美洲並試飲那種飲料時，歐洲人才首度知道巧克力的存在。

雖然把巧克力引進歐洲的是西班牙人，但法國、英國與荷蘭等國很快就開始在他們的殖民地上種植可可。隨著供給增加，價格下滑，一般大眾也可以享用這種美味的飲品。大家開始實驗，沒多久巧克力也出現在糕餅中。1828 年，當荷蘭巧克力製造商康拉德・范・侯頓 (Conrad J. van Houten) 發現有更簡單的方法可以製作巧克力粉時，才真正掀起世界的「巧克力風潮」。

根據侯頓的技術，英國巧克力製造商喬瑟夫・斯托爾斯・佛賴 (Joseph Storrs Fry) 重新混合可可粉與可可脂，在 1847 年製作出第一塊食用的巧克力。可可脂是一種天然的脂肪，每顆可可豆內含約 54% 的可可脂。如今深受大家喜愛的巧克力牛奶，則是瑞士的亨利・奈斯透 (Henri Nestle，雀巢) 率先混合奶粉及其他原料所發明的。

1. 本文主要是關於 ＿＿＿＿ 。
   (A) 可可粉如何以更簡單的方法製造
   (B) 巧克力如何對西班牙來說是賺錢的工業
   (C) 巧克力的簡史
   (D) 巧克力的療效
   本文談巧克力自西元 500 年至今的歷史。

2. 第一段中的 "boost" 這個字最適合以 ＿＿＿＿ 替代？
   (A) 忍受　**(B) 增加**　(C) 減少　(D) 區別
   線索就在同一句的 increase。

3. 誰找出製作可可粉最簡單的方法並把它介紹給全世界？
   (A) 康拉德・范・侯頓
   (B) 喬瑟夫・斯托爾斯・佛賴
   (C) 亨利・奈斯透
   (D) 赫南多・科爾特斯
   見第四段最後一句。

4. 歐洲人在 ＿＿＿＿ 開始知道巧克力。
   (A) 1828 年
   (B) 16 世紀中葉
   (C) 1849 年
   (D) 哥倫布發現美洲那年
   見第三段第一句。

5. 依據本文，以下何者不實？
   (A) 並非所有阿茲特克人都可以取得巧克力。
   (B) 馬雅人最早用壓碎的可可豆做成飲料。
   (C) 歐洲國家在殖民地種可可樹，結果供應增加而價格就降低了。
   (D) 一家英國巧克力公司發明一種方法把巧克力加入牛奶，製成了大家熟知的巧克力牛奶。
   見第五段最後一句。

boost	v.	提高	reserve	v.	保留	warrior	n.	戰士
voyage	n.	航行	cultivate	v.	種植	colony	n.	殖民地
the masses		大眾	pastry	n.	糕餅	invasion	n.	入侵

1993 年，建築師大衛・馬克斯 (David Marks) 與茱莉亞・巴菲爾德 (Julia Barfield) 第一次繪製倫敦眼。他們參加英國舉行的比賽，想在 20 世紀結束之際建造千禧地標。不幸的是，沒人得獎，專案完全取消了。不過，馬克斯與巴菲爾德並不願放棄，他們持續進行計畫，實現他們為下一世紀創作「高聳之作」的夢想。他們的夢想引起了大眾關注。在英國航空的資助下，倫敦眼終於完成了，於 2000 年 3 月對外開放。從此倫敦就一直是眾所矚目的焦點。

倫敦眼——有時又稱為千禧輪——狀似巨型單車輪。上面掛著 32 個乘客座艙。人們搭上座艙便升空 135 米。由於轉輪旋轉地非常緩慢，所以不需要停下來讓乘客登上座艙。每個座艙旋轉一圈大約要 30 分鐘。轉輪每天可搭載 15,000 名觀光客，可旋轉約 22 圈。

倫敦眼之所以是倫敦市的首要觀光景點，原因很簡單。因為它就矗立在倫敦市中心，可以讓遊客欣賞城市的驚人美景。從每個座艙上，遊客可向四方放眼 25 英里，所以可以輕易看到白金漢宮、聖保羅大教堂、西敏寺等等全球知名的倫敦地標。遊客還可以租用附空調的座艙開私人派對。每個座艙最多可容納 25 人——足以開個舒適的聚會，同時享用美酒、佳餚與美景。

拉斯維加斯及上海等其他城市正計畫超越倫敦眼，不過倫敦眼將永遠拔得頭籌。

1. 倫敦眼主要是建造來 _____。
   (A) 紀念千禧年
   (B) 創新紀錄
   (C) 提供新的遊樂場所
   (D) 使競爭激烈
   見第一段第二句。

2. 乘客旋轉一圈要多久？
   (A) 15 分鐘。　　　　(B) 22 分鐘。
   (C) 25 分鐘。　　　　(D) 30 分鐘。
   見第二段倒數第二句。

3. 第三段 "accommodate" 這個字最適合以 _____ 替代。
   (A) 擠滿　(B) 娛樂　(C) 防衛　(D) 容納

4. 倫敦眼不用停下讓乘客搭乘是因為 _____。
   (A) 它一開始旋轉就停不下來
   (B) 它轉得很慢所以乘客很容易搭乘
   (C) 這樣可以節省更多的能源
   (D) 這樣會讓乘客覺得更刺激
   見第二段第四句。

5. 依據此文下列何者不實？
   (A) 倫敦眼受歡迎的原因之一是遊客可以從倫敦市中心欣賞美景。
   (B) 乘客在搭乘倫敦眼時，可以看到 25 英里遠的地標。
   (C) 由英航設計的倫敦眼於 1993 年開始建造。
   (D) 倫敦眼包含 32 個有空調的座艙。
   見第一段第一句和倒數第二句。

architect n. 建築師	millennium n. 千禧年	capsule n. 座艙
rotate v. 旋轉	sightseer n. 觀光客	premiere adj. 第一的
cathedral n. 大教堂	accommodate v. 容納	outdo v. 超越

蘭斯・阿姆斯壯 (Lance Armstrong) 於 1971 年生於德州,從青少年開始就是有天賦的運動員。他一開始原本是鐵人三項的選手,但沒多久就把注意力轉到業餘單車上。他開始參賽,1992 年加入美國奧運代表隊,後來才變成職業選手。他首度參加職業賽(聖賽巴斯提安菁英賽)成績墊底後,就決定不再讓這種事情發生。

他接著開始贏得比賽,打響名聲。不幸的是,1996 年當他比完一場比賽下車時,感到一陣疼痛。結果是睪丸癌,診斷時已幾乎蔓延全身。醫師對他的病情並不樂觀,但是他接受 3 年的治療後竟然戲劇性地活下來了。

1999 年,他東山再起,首度贏得環法自行車大賽,後來連續六年蟬聯奪冠。他不僅獲獎,更成為一個傳奇。有些人把環法自行車大賽稱為「蘭斯大賽」以表達對蘭斯・阿姆斯壯的敬意。他從此便從比賽中退休了,但並未就此歇息。他除了投入慈善工作,為大眾的癌症認知及研究募款之外,他也參與電影的演出。

他不僅是堅強的人,也是青年人的楷模。他在著作《重返豔陽下》(*It's Not About the Bike*) 中提到,當他 100 歲時,他想騎車衝下阿爾卑斯山,看大家為他的成功加油,到時他就可以躺在美麗的法國田野間,優雅長眠。

1. 蘭斯・阿姆斯壯贏得環法自行車大賽 _____。
   (A) 從 1999 年到 2004 年連續 6 次
   (B) 從 1992 年到 1997 年連續 6 次
   (C) 從 1999 年到 2005 年連續 7 次
   (D) 從 1997 年到 2002 年連續 7 次

見第三段第一句。

2. 當蘭斯・阿姆斯壯完成首次職業賽時,他可能是 _____。
   (A) 很懷疑的
   (B) 很有決心的
   (C) 很沮喪的
   (D) 很挫折的
   見第一段最後一句。

3. 下列哪一項有關蘭斯・阿姆斯壯得癌症的敘述是錯誤的?
   (A) 他在 1996 年被診斷罹患睪丸癌。
   (B) 他得知罹癌時,癌細胞已擴散至全身。
   (C) 經過 3 年的治療,他康復了,並回到自行車界。
   (D) 醫生告訴他存活機率很大。
   見第二段最後一句。

4. 第三段"trophy"這個字很可能是一項 _____。
   (A) 好處　**(B) 獎品**　(C) 挫敗　(D) 障礙
   線索在上一句,敘述他贏了比賽。

5. 下列哪一項在原文中未敘述?
   (A) 阿姆斯壯以鐵人三項開始運動生涯。
   (B) 阿姆斯壯籌募基金來支持癌症研究並且喚起人們對癌症的認知。
   (C) 阿姆斯壯在 1997 年成立蘭斯・阿姆斯壯基金會。
   (D) 阿姆斯壯想要在 100 歲時再贏得一次勝利,然後在法國田野間優雅地死去。

athlete　n.　運動員	triathlete　n.　鐵人三項的選手	amateur　adj.　業餘的
testicular　adj.　睪丸的	diagnose　v.　診斷	comeback　n.　復出
trophy　n.　獎品,獎杯	legend　n.　傳奇	the Alps　阿爾卑斯山

你知道如今有些手術是由機器外科醫生而非真人醫生所施行的嗎？這些外科醫生是由機器開發而成，用來進行人類雙手難以處理的特定手術，因為這些手術需要很多細小、精準的動作。

大多數的機器外科醫生，例如「達文西外科手術系統」，並不會完全取代醫生，而是協助真人醫生進行更精確的手術。「達文西」是由四支手臂的機器人及「檢視控制台」所組成，檢視控制台是一個有控制面板的電視螢幕。機器外科醫生的三支手臂握著手術器材，第四支手臂內建攝影機，把影像傳送到「檢視控制台」。在隔壁房內的真人醫生藉此觀察電視螢幕上的影像並指引機器人。

並非所有人都認同使用機器外科醫生的好處。有些人擔心機器人犯錯時無法自覺，認為人腦還是比機器可靠。他們尤其擔心未來機器人會在毫無真人醫生的參與下進行手術的預言。其他人則指出機器的成本高昂，而且訓練人員使用機器還需要花費額外的時間與金錢。

不過，機器手術是迅速成長的領域。支持者表示，最重要的優點是機器手臂不會像人的手一樣顫動。所以它可以進行更快、更精確的手術。這表示每天可以進行更多的手術，成功率更高。在新的系統年年推陳出新之下，機器外科醫生即使受到批評，似乎真的會是未來的外科醫生。

1. 本文的主要目的是 _____。
   (A) 介紹機器外科醫生
   (B) 介紹達文西外科手術系統
   (C) 討論機器手術的好處
   (D) 討論機器手術的壞處
   本文主要介紹機器外科醫生(包含優缺點)。

2. 下列哪一項有關達文西外科手術系統的敘述是不正確的？
   (A) 它由一個機器人和一個檢視控制台組成。
   (B) 在檢視控制台看到的影像是從連結在其中一個機械臂上的攝影機傳送的。
   (C) 它可以完全取代真人外科醫生。
   (D) 檢視操作台設立在手術室隔壁的房間裡。
   見第二段第一句。

3. 依據本文，下列哪一項是使用外科手術用機器人的主要理由？
   (A) 較長的手術時間。
   (B) 較短的恢復時間。
   (C) 方便性。
   (D) 精確性。
   見第一段最後一句和最後一段二、三句。

4. 在本文中未提到下列哪一項人們對機器人手術的憂心？
   (A) 外科手術用機器人太貴。
   (B) 機器手術比傳統手術費時。
   (C) 未來外科手術用機器人將會完全取代真人外科醫生。
   (D) 醫生和護士學習使用這種機器人需要額外的時間和金錢。
   見第三段。

5. 作者對機器外科醫生的態度為何？
   (A) 贊成。　　　　(B) 反對。
   (C) 中立。　　　　(D) 妥協。
   見最後一段。

precise adj. 精確的	surgical adj. 外科手術的	console n. 控制台
panel n. 儀表板	staff n. 工作人員	critic n. 批評者

數獨又名「數字填空」，是美國建築師及猜謎遊戲設計者霍華德・格昂斯 (Howard Garns) 最先發明的。1970 年代末期，《戴爾雜誌》首度在紐約刊登這種謎題。1984 年，一家日本謎題公司把它引進日本。它馬上在日本掀起熱潮，後來命名為數獨，在日語中意指「單獨的數字」。

1997 年，退休的香港法官韋恩・古德 (Wayne Gould) 在東京的書店偶然發現數獨謎題。他花了 6 年的時間開發一套可以迅速產生謎題的電腦軟體。後來他把軟體賣給《泰晤士報》。2004 年 11 月 12 日，倫敦報紙上第一次出現數獨謎題，從此以後便天天刊登。幾個月後，其他多種英國報紙也開始刊登他們自己的數獨謎題。2005 年 4 月，謎題紅回紐約，數獨熱潮迅速蔓延全美。

如今，數獨已然變成一種全球運動。有數獨社團、書籍與網站。現在除了用紙筆外，在手機或電腦上也可以玩數獨遊戲，甚至還有數獨比賽！2006 年 3 月 10 日至 12 日，第一屆世界數獨冠軍大賽在義大利舉行。有 85 人參加比賽，由捷克會計師珍納・泰洛法 (Jana Tylova) 獲得冠軍。她表示：「我喜歡數獨，因為你只需要一張紙、一枝筆，運用一點邏輯思考和耐心就行了。」

沒有人可以否認，這種超人氣的謎題深受各年齡層的喜愛，可以提供腦部運動。有些學校還拿數獨謎題給學生練習，鼓勵他們動腦思考。有些專家甚至建議老年人玩數獨遊戲，以避免阿滋海默症及失憶。

1. 依據本文，解出數獨謎題需要 _____。
   (A) 邏輯和耐性

   (B) 新的電腦設備
   (C) 進階的數學能力
   (D) 快速的計算
   見第三段最後一句。

2. 多少年後數獨又回到美國而且很受歡迎？
   (A) 大約 11 年。　　(B) 大約 15 年。
   (C) 大約 30 年。　　(D) 大約 50 年。
   見第一段第二句和第二段第六句。

3. 數獨起源於 _____。
   (A) 美國　　　　　(B) 日本
   (C) 英國　　　　　(D) 義大利
   見第一段一、二句。

4. 依據本文，下列何者不實？
   (A) 2006 年，世界各地的數獨愛好者首次有機會在義大利挑戰彼此。
   (B) 今天數獨風潮已經傳遍世界各地。
   (C) 數獨傳進日本後很快就大受歡迎。
   (D) 韋恩・古德花了 8 年時間發展電腦程式來快速設計謎題。
   見第二段第二句。

5. 醫生建議老年人玩數獨是因為它可以 _____。
   (A) 增強閱讀能力
   (B) 刺激思考
   (C) 使他們比年輕人有耐性
   (D) 很容易解答
   見最後一段最後兩句 (stimulate thinking、Alzheimer's disease 和 memory loss)。

architect n. 建築師	craze n. 風潮	global adj. 全球的
phenomenon n. 現象	mobile phone 行動電話	competition n. 競賽
adopt v. 採用	stimulate v. 刺激	

刺青一詞源於大溪地語 *tatau*，意指「標記」。刺青始於史前時代，當時的人利用刺青辨識部落或家族、標示罪犯、防止各種疾病及崇拜神明。18 世紀末期，庫克船長由南太平洋返回倫敦時，帶回一位全身多處刺青的玻里尼西亞人，名叫歐麥 (Omai)。他造成了轟動，刺青很快就變成英國上流社會間所流傳的風潮。

美國內戰期間，士兵為了紀念死去的袍澤及軍旅生涯而刺青。不過一直等到 1891 年，紐約的山繆爾‧歐萊里 (Samuel O'Reilly) 發明電動刺青機以後，刺青才在普羅大眾間廣為流行。刺青的普遍流行則導致上流社會將之拒於門外。許多罪犯利用刺青記錄他們的罪行與刑罰。這種刺青文化讓很多人把刺青和犯罪聯想在一起。

20 世紀中葉，刺青依舊給人很差的印象。因為報紙報導了感染肝炎的案例，甚至讓刺青被認為很危險，人氣也下滑。不過，在 60 年代末期，由於很多名人也開始刺青，於是大家便對刺青大為改觀。深諳媒體操作的美國人萊爾‧坦特 (Lyle Tuttle) 把刺青這種地下藝術變成主流。如今有愈來愈多的人跟隨這股風潮。

在刺青之前，有很多事情必須先做好考慮。日後如果想要去除刺青是相當痛苦的，而花費可能比刺青本身還高。而且刺青還可能傳播愛滋病與 B 型及 C 型肝炎等血源感染疾病。

1. 史前時代人們刺青的理由有好幾種，除了 _____ 之外。

(A) 健康　**(B) 藝術**　(C) 宗教　(D) 文化

見第一段第二句，並未提到藝術的理由。

2. 第一段 "sensation" 這個字最適合以 _____ 替代？

(A) 恐慌　(B) 障礙　**(C) 轟動**　(D) 防衛

線索是下一行的 **craze** (風潮)。

3. 第二段 "them" 這個代名詞指涉 _____。

(A) 刺青

(B) 許多人

(C) 犯罪

(D) 入監服刑

4. 依據本文，以下何者不實？

(A) 現在刺青受歡迎的程度提升。

(B) 歐麥被庫克船長引見到倫敦。

(C) 20 世紀中葉，刺青因為會感染肝炎而不受到歡迎。

(D) 萊爾‧坦特發明了第一個電動刺青的機器。

見第二段第二句。

5. 從本文可以類推出 _____。

(A) 二次大戰期間歐洲的軍人熱衷刺青

(B) 歐洲皇室成員都不刺青

(C) 20 世紀初期，刺青藝術家受到大眾尊敬

(D) 電動刺青的機器發明之前，刺青在上流社會受到歡迎

見第二段第三句。

tattoo n. 刺青	originate v. 起源	prehistoric adj. 史前的
criminal n. 罪犯	idolize v. 崇拜	sensation n. 轟動
comrade n. 戰友	hepatitis n. 肝炎	mainstream n. 主流

很多人認為滑雪板是比較現代的運動，由想在冬天玩滑板的青少年所發明與促使流行的。不過，滑雪板的歷史實際上溯及 1929 年，當時首度出現類似滑雪板的裝置。

第一塊「滑雪板」是名為傑克‧柏契特 (Jack Burchett) 的人所發明的，他試圖用曬衣繩把腳固定在一片合板上，以便滑雪下山。這種基本模式持續了三十幾年，直到這個運動的下一個重要階段開始為止。1965 年，雪曼‧波本 (Sherman Poppen) 為女兒發明了 Snurfer 做為玩具。他把兩片滑雪屐綁在一起，並在前端加裝一條繩子操控方向。他很快就照著這個想法生產，往後十年總共賣出一百萬台 Snurfer。

從那時起，雪地滑板已歷經多種變化，例如加裝了固定裝置，用來讓滑板者固定在滑板上。滑板形狀也各異。雖然滑雪板的概念已經被採用了近 80 年，但是直到最近 15 年來，這項運動才真正受到熱愛冬季運動的人喜愛。

雪地滑板運動在 1988 年冬季奧運會第一次登上重要國際舞台。雖然很多滑雪者並不喜歡和滑板者共用滑道的主意，但是在全世界各大滑雪勝地看到滑板者已經變得很平常了。現在雪地滑板的接受度比以前更高，每年都有五百多萬冬季運動迷在坡道上玩滑板。滑雪者，小心囉！雪地滑板會就此長存。

1. 在第二階段的滑雪板出現之前，有 _____ 年之久柏契特的滑雪板一直是基本樣版。
   (A) 10　**(B) 30**　(C) 40　(D) 80
   見第二段第二句。

2. 自從 _____ 以來，滑雪板已經真正受到冬季運動愛好者的歡迎。

(A) **90 年代初期**
(B) 60 年代末期
(C) 1965 年
(D) 1938 年
見第三段最後一句。

3. 波本 _____ 來製造 "Snurfer" 滑雪板。
   (A) 使用一塊合板，用曬衣繩把腳固定住在板子上
   (B) 把兩塊硬木板綁在一起，並用線繫在前端
   (C) 把兩個滑雪屐綁在一起，並用繩索繫在前端
   (D) 把硬紙板黏在合板上面
   見第二段倒數第二句。

4. 本文最後一句的意思是？
   (A) 滑雪板已經普遍而且永遠被接受。
   (B) 滑雪板裝備可能會更貴。
   (C) 雪地滑板和滑雪一樣危險。
   (D) 玩滑雪板並保持年輕。

5. 依據本文，下列何者不實？
   (A) Snurfer 滑雪板是第一個行銷的滑雪板。
   (B) 現在大多數的冬季度假勝地都不接受雪地滑板者。
   (C) Snurfer 滑雪板最初是波本做給女兒當玩具的。
   (D) 1998 年滑雪板首次出現在冬季奧運會中。
   見第四段第二句。

device　n.　裝置	secure　v.　弄牢	plywood　n.　合板
clothesline　n.　曬衣繩	steer　v.　操控	binding　n.　固定裝置
slope　n.　斜坡	ski resort　滑雪勝地	

外星人意外？
Alien Accidents?

1947 年 7 月，在新墨西哥州的沙漠上，一位牧場工人發現長四分之三英里、寬數百英尺的區域上散佈著大量不尋常的殘骸。他向羅斯威爾 (Roswell) 的美國空軍報案。他們很快便進行調查並發佈新聞稿，表示他們發現了一架墜毀的飛碟及外星人遺體。這個新聞震驚了全國。

但是新聞發佈 4 小時以後，說法就變了：原本以為是飛碟的東西事實上是氣象探測氣球。由於美國政府先承認發現外星人遺體，後來又予以否認，所以更多人開始相信這是真的，認為政府試圖隱瞞某些事情。

50 年後，當美國政府證實所謂的外星人遺體是高度機密研究專案所使用的測試假人時，這個案件才終告結案。不管案子如何，幽浮熱開始流行，幽浮目擊報告變成一種流行文化。大家認為幽浮是造成許多神秘事件的原因，例如麥田圈，甚或是百慕達三角洲內的消失事件。

很多人認為幽浮和外星人是真的，他們也相信外太空有高智慧生物存在的可能性。其他人在毫無具體證據下往往抱持著懷疑的態度。可惜的是，如果有任何幽浮或外星人存在的證據，大眾都不得而知。你相信他們的存在嗎？在我們獲得更好、更可靠的證據之前，答案仍然懸而未決。

1. 本文主旨為何？
(A) 民眾認為美國政府對於羅斯威爾事件撒謊。
(B) 羅斯威爾事件引起人們對幽浮存在的興趣。
(C) 多數人認為外星人和幽浮是存在的。
(D) 人們相信百慕達三角洲是外星人設的陷阱。

本文先介紹羅斯威爾事件，再談此事件之後人們開始對幽浮和外星人產生興趣。

2. 美國空軍何時發表結案報告，說所謂的外星人屍體其實是測試假人？
(A) 1947 年。　　　(B) 1974 年。
(C) 1994 年。　　　**(D) 1997 年。**
見第三段第一句。

3. 依據本文，下列哪一項有關羅斯威爾事件是正確的？
(A) 幽浮在 1974 年 7 月墜落在新墨西哥的一條河流裡。
(B) 一個牧場工人發現外星人屍體並且向美國空軍報告。
(C) 政府在接獲事件報告不久之後就開始調查。
(D) 空軍最早的聲明是說所謂的外星人屍體只是軍事用的假人。
見第一段第三句。

4. 美國政府對羅斯威爾事件的態度讓更多人相信政府企圖 _____。
(A) 掩飾真相和隱瞞已被發現的事
(B) 保護美國人不受外星人攻擊
(C) 揭發他們偉大的發現
(D) 暗示外太空的生命形式確實存在
見第二段第二句。

5. 作者對幽浮和外星人的存在可能是什麼態度？
(A) 正面的。　　　(B) 冷淡的。
(C) 懷疑的。　　　**(D) 中立的。**
線索在本文最後兩句。

| rancher | n. | 農場工人／主人 | debris | n. | 殘骸 | issue | v. | 發佈 |
| dummy | n. | 假人 | mania | n. | 狂熱 | triangle | n. | 三角形(之物) |

每年八月的最後一個星期三，成千上萬的人湧入西班牙布諾爾 (Buñol) 的街上慶祝蕃茄節。

蕃茄節的起源至少有兩種說法。其中一種是，有一個男人演奏的音樂很難聽，他的朋友決定開他玩笑，拿蕃茄砸他。另一種說法是大家認為比較可靠與正確的版本，在 1945 年有些年輕人從鎮上廣場裡的菜販那拿走蕃茄，並用蕃茄打打鬧鬧。

隔年的同一天，這些年輕人又再度聚集，帶蕃茄來打鬧。警察制止了他們，而布諾爾鎮直到 1950 年才允許蕃茄大戰。後來由於其他不願參與的人遭到攻擊才又再度被阻止。到了 1959 年，布諾爾人要求鎮公所允許舉辦蕃茄節；這次為了避免意外與攻擊還訂了一些規矩。當地政府希望節慶維持一貫有趣的精神。

如今這些規矩依舊適用，它們也證實是防止傷害的有效方法。例如，參與者不可以拉扯別人的衣服，節慶過後不可以丟蕃茄，還有不可以攜帶瓶子或其他危險物品。當然，最重要的規定是，所有蕃茄在拋出去以前都必須先壓碎，才不會傷人。

如果沒有蕃茄節，很少人會知道布諾爾這個城鎮。如今，大家從世界各地紛湧而至，只為了參加這個罕見與難忘的活動。

1. 蕃茄節終於在 _____ 受到官方認可，並持續在每年舉行，一直到現在。
(A) 1950　　　　(B) 1945
(C) 1959　　　(D) 1969
見第三段第四行。

2. 第二段的代名詞 "them" 指涉 _____。

(A) 年輕人　　　　**(B) 蕃茄**
(C) 小販　　　　　(D) 說法

3. 本文最可能出自 _____。
(A) 農業雜誌　　　**(B) 旅遊雜誌**
(C) 歷史報告　　　(D) 消費指南
原文介紹這個吸引世界各地遊客的節慶，很可能是旅遊雜誌的報導。

4. 可以推測此節慶被禁止舉行好幾年是因為 _____。
(A) 蕃茄供應短缺
(B) 當地人會攻擊陌生人
(C) 鎮公所會太髒而無法清洗
(D) 有關當局害怕情況會失控
見第三段第三句，因為有人攻擊不參加者，而不是(B)選項說的陌生人。

5. 依據本文，下列何者不實？
(A) 節慶於八月最後一個星期三在西班牙布諾爾舉行。
(B) 一宣佈結束，參加的人就要停止扔蕃茄。
(C) 舉行此節慶不僅是因為好玩而且有其宗教意義。
(D) 一般人認為此節慶起源於 1945 年，一群年輕人在廣場打了起來。
本文並未提到此節慶有宗教意義。

origin　n. 起源	accurate　adj. 精確的	version　n. 說法
vendor　n. 小販	owing to　由於	maintain　v. 維持
participant　n. 參加者	crush　v. 壓碎	

　　我們通常都不喜歡被回嘴。不過，對鸚鵡就另當別論了。

　　鸚鵡以會說話出名，但是實際上牠們並沒有聲帶。而是擁有比其他鳥類更長、更發達的舌頭，對於調整聲音很重要。牠們控制喉嚨的肌肉，讓舌頭前後移動而藉此發聲。看到鸚鵡把鳥嘴張得更開以便發出「一」的聲音很有趣。雖然鸚鵡可以按正確的用字順序說幾句話，但是牠們無法像人類一樣運用語法。所以，牠們普遍不被認為真的擁有說話能力。

　　不過，許多科學家與寵物主認為，鸚鵡說話時，牠們是在和人類溝通。愛琳・派珀格 (Irene Pepperberg) 教授一直以來都是和鸚鵡工作，她相信鸚鵡的智慧。她表示，有些鸚鵡的智力可以和 3 到 5 歲的幼童相比。以她最老的非洲灰鸚鵡艾力克斯 (Alex) 為例。過去 27 年來，她一直教牠一些複雜的任務。牠可以用一百個字彙說話，甚至還可以思考。教授說艾力克斯的動作不單是本能反應而已，而是推理與選擇的結果。此外，牠還會分辨顏色與形狀，辨識 50 種不同的物件。牠也知道相同與不同的概念。

　　如果你想教鸚鵡說話，切記鸚鵡是透過與主人之間的一對一關係來學習說話。訓練牠們說話時，和牠們保持良好的關係一向很有幫助。試著和牠們建立口語習慣。讚美也能對鸚鵡說話產生神奇的作用。

1. 下列何者鸚鵡發出聲音時不會用到？
　(A) **聲帶。**　　　　(B) 喉嚨。
　(C) 舌頭。　　　　(D) 鳥嘴。
　見第二段前四句。

2. 有些人認為鸚鵡不能夠真正說話是因為 ＿＿＿＿。
　(A) 他們不能說一個完整的句子
　(B) **他們不可能以人類語言的複雜形式說話**
　(C) 他們不能和人類用同樣的方式發出聲音
　(D) 人類不喜歡被回嘴
　見第二段最後兩句。

3. 根據本文，下列哪一項有關艾力克斯的敘述是不正確的？
　(A) 愛琳・派珀格教他有 20 多年了。
　(B) **他不能把相同顏色或形狀的物體歸類。**
　(C) 他可以對主人的命令有反應而且執行某些工作。
　(D) 他的行為是根據推理的。
　見第三段倒數兩句。

4. 教鸚鵡說話的時候，建議主人要避免 ＿＿＿＿。
　(A) **同時教兩隻鸚鵡**
　(B) 和他們建立良好的關係
　(C) 獎賞他們的好表現
　(D) 每天早上要對他們說早安
　見最後一段第一句。

5. 第三段 "rival" 這個字最適合以 ＿＿＿＿ 取代。
　(A) 打擊　　　　　(B) 使榮耀
　(C) **比得上**　　　　(D) 使變壞
　線索在這個句子中拿鸚鵡的智力和小孩的智力來相比。

vocal cord	聲帶	tongue	n. 舌頭	modify	v. 調整
beak	n. 鳥嘴	syntax	n. 語法	rival	v. 比得上
instinctive	adj. 直覺的	reasoning	n. 推理	routine	n. 習慣

12 永遠寫部落格
Blogging for Good

網路上三千八百萬個部落格中，有 52.8% 是由青少年架設與維護的。在青少年的部落格上可以看到什麼？或許是他或她的藝術作品、與學校有關的事、最愛的歌曲與電影、抱怨、以及關於生活的隨想。簡言之，部落格可以寫關於任何青少年能用來向他人傳達自我的東西。

青少年部落客用他們的網站來表達自我，接觸朋友、家人與外在世界。青少年藉由上網揭露自己以尋找志同道合的人。他們試圖尋找一種歸屬感。

很多人認為網路日誌實際上有一些優點。例如，寫部落格似乎可以提高讀寫能力。每天更新部落格的青少年不就是在天天寫文章嗎？那對他或她的寫作技巧絕對有很大的幫助。此外，青少年還可以藉由表達自我而獲得滿足感。另一個寫部落格影響深遠的例子，是它提高了青少年的社會認知。他們有些人不僅把個人的經驗貼上網路，也鼓勵其他青少年走出去，參與對抗世界飢荒、童工等活動。此外，家長藉由瀏覽子女每日更新的文章，可以更了解他們的後代。部落格肯定能比尷尬的晚餐對話透露更多的訊息。

家長與老師可能是對的：寫部落格可能是危險的。但是部落格在多方面對現在的青少年都有幫助，這可能促使我們讓青少年持久在部落格上寫下去。

1. 本文的主旨為何？
   (A) 部落格非常受青少年歡迎。
   (B) 部落格是青少年自我療癒的方式。
   (C) 部落格有助青少年開發並維持社交關係。
   (D) **青少年湧向部落格並從中獲益許多。**
   文章談青少年喜愛部落格並從中獲益。

2. 以下哪一個青少年部落格的好處未在本文中提及？
   (A) **擴展青少年對未來的觀點。**
   (B) 增進青少年的寫作能力。
   (C) 發展青少年的社會認知。
   (D) 獲得滿足感。
   見第三段第四、五、六句。

3. 本文中未提到以下列哪一項青少年使用部落格的目的？
   (A) 表達自我。　　(B) 與人有所關聯。
   (C) **炫耀技術。**　　(D) 尋求認同。
   第二、三段未提到炫耀技術。

4. 第三段 "offspring" 這個字可以以 ＿＿＿＿ 替代。
   (A) 青少年　　　(B) 勞工
   (C) 部落客　　　(D) **孩子**
   線索在同一句的「孩子」。

5. 作者對青少年部落客的態度為何？
   (A) **贊成。**　　　(B) 反對。
   (C) 中立。　　　(D) 冷淡。
   線索在最後一段第二句。

cyberspace　n.　網路空間　　　random　adj.　隨機的　　　a sense of belonging　歸屬感
boost　v.　提高　　　literacy　n.　讀寫能力　　　offspring　n.　後代

歡笑是最佳良藥
Laughter is the Best Medicine

馬里蘭大學最近做的一項研究顯示，歡笑可以避免心臟病。研究人員發現，心臟病患者和同年齡沒有心臟病的人相比，在多種情況下比較不可能會笑。

不過，這些研究人員還不知道為什麼歡笑可以保護心臟。或許是因為歡笑會在體內釋放保護性的化學物質，或是因為它可以運動心臟與肺臟，因而增加血液中的含氧量。研究團隊的隊長米勒 (Miller) 博士表示：「我們知道運動可以降低心臟病的風險。或許經常開懷大笑也應該加入這個清單之中。」

歡笑的另一個好處是可以藉由增加可攻擊病毒、外來細胞與癌細胞的 T 細胞數目，來增強免疫系統。再者，歡笑也會增加 B 細胞，產生摧毀疾病的抗體。歡笑也可以降低血壓及抒解壓力。

一般也認為歡笑可以幫助經歷痛苦療程或因為預期痛苦而感到焦慮的病患。這是因為歡笑可以讓身體釋放天然的止痛劑，因而暫時忘卻疼痛。有些兒童醫院會派專業的小丑醫師進入兒童病房，注入一點歡樂。他們不是醫生，而是喬裝成小丑的演員。他們的任務很簡單，卻有很正面的效果。歡笑不僅不用花費就有益健康，還沒有不良的副作用。

1. 本文的主要目的是 ＿＿＿＿。
   (A) 探索米勒博士有關歡笑的理論。
   (B) 說明歡笑對疼痛的效果。
   (C) 說明歡笑對健康的好處。
   (D) 描述壓力如何影響健康。
   全文都在舉證說明歡笑對健康的好處(包含消除疼痛)。

2. 在兒童醫院中小丑醫師做些什麼事？
   (A) 他們幫醫師處理疼痛的治療。
   (B) 他們協助護理人員幫兒童人打針。
   (C) 他們和小孩的父母談歡笑的好處。
   (D) 他們運用技巧以歡笑治療病童。
   見第四段第三句。

3. 米勒博士和他的團員發現 ＿＿＿＿。
   (A) 歡笑有助於放鬆緊張的肌肉
   (B) 壓力似乎是頭號殺手
   (C) 歡笑讓人忘掉了疼痛
   (D) 有心臟病的人通常比較少笑
   見第一段第二句。

4. 第四段 "distraction" 這個字的指的是 ＿＿＿＿ 的東西。
   (A) 轉移人們注意力
   (B) 可以增加總數
   (C) 令人擔心
   (D) 令人滿足
   線索在同一句的前半部。

5. 依據本文，下列何者不實？
   (A) 米勒博士很清楚地瞭解歡笑為何有助於預防心臟病。
   (B) 至今仍未發現歡笑有負面的副作用。
   (C) 大笑可以增加攻擊病毒的細胞數量。
   (D) 為了心臟健康我們應該規律運動、吃正確的食物、多笑。
   見第二段第一句。

chemical	n.	化學物質	
distraction	n.	分散注意力的事物	
oxygen	n.	氧氣	
ward	n.	病房	
immune system		免疫系統	
inject	v.	注射，注入	

可口可樂公司
The Coca-Cola Company

可口可樂是世界上最受歡迎的飲料。該公司的特色是促銷商品的天賦，再結合持續擴張市場的動力。

早在 1886 年，亞特蘭大藥劑師約翰·潘伯頓 (John Pemberton) 發明原始配方後沒幾個月，可口可樂就在美國的地方性報紙上刊登廣告宣傳。他把可口可樂當成治療頭痛的藥水銷售，不過標語簡潔有力：「暢飲可口可樂。」

1892 年成立可口可樂公司後，隨之而來的就是全國性的擴張。該公司在亞特蘭大以外的地區建立裝瓶場，以便讓可口可樂的消費擴散至全美各州。這項擴張還搭配可口可樂在全美各地穀倉門及建築邊牆所打的廣告，還聘請知名歌手、演員、運動明星促銷可口可樂。特製的可口可樂月曆、盤子與瓶子也有助於建立品牌。

20 世紀，可口可樂往海外擴張。從 1920 年代開始，該公司就密集地以世界各地城市的電子招牌向大家放送可口可樂商標的圖案。可口可樂利用新式大眾媒體，在收音機與電視上打廣告，創造出「就是可口可樂！」(1982) 之類的標語。1971 年，一支知名的電視廣告播送一大群不同種族的年輕人聚在山頂高唱「我想請全世界喝瓶可樂」，道盡可口可樂進軍全球的野心。該公司也贊助奧運及世界盃足球賽等主要運動賽事。

可口可樂公司維持其動力與遠見，持續追求新的市場，以確保「世界各地各個角落」都有可口可樂。

1. 本文的主要目的是描述 _____。
   (A) 為何世界各地的人都喜歡可口可樂

   (B) 可口可樂如何在無意中發明
   (C) 可口可樂如何成功地推銷和行銷
   (D) 為何此公司的標語可以吸引消費者的興趣
   全文都在談此公司如何運用不同的方法行銷。

2. 可口可樂最早的配方 _____。
   (A) 是由當地記者發明的
   (B) 有其療效
   (C) 在 1892 年發明
   (D) 立刻在全世界受到歡迎
   見第二段第二句。

3. 以下哪一項未在本文中被敘述為 1920 年代之前可口可樂能夠傳遍全美各地的理由？
   (A) 亞特蘭大外設立了裝瓶工廠。
   (B) 很多名人幫忙推銷可口可樂。
   (C) 可口可樂透過電子廣告招牌推銷。
   (D) 全國的消費者喜歡它特別製造的產品。
   (C)選項提到的是 1920 年代以後在世界各地的宣傳方式。

4. 第一段 "coupled" 這個字最適合以 _____ 替代。
   (A) 傳達 **(B) 結合** (C) 比較 (D) 充滿

5. 第四段 "the new mass media" 這幾個字指的是 _____。
   (A) 電視和網路
   (B) 收音機和戶外廣告
   (C) 收音機和報紙
   (D) 收音機和電視
   線索在第四段第二句這些字之後。

couple v. 結合　　　　pharmacist n. 藥劑師　　　　nationwide adj. 全國性的
consumption n. 消費　　bombard v. 砲轟　　　　　sponsor v. 贊助

治療用動物又名治療用寵物，大多以狗居多，但也可以包括貓、兔子、甚至是鳥類。成為勝任的治療用動物需要有特定的性格特質。牠們必須喜歡人類、溫和、可掌控，最重要的是，要有穩定的性格。這些基本特質讓治療用動物受到人的輕撫或觸摸時，能夠安靜與發揮耐心。

這些人與動物的短暫互動對人的健康有好處。雖然沒有實驗室的資料可以顯示與動物互動如何影響人的身體，但科學研究顯示，人在接觸治療用動物後表示，他們比較不覺得寂寞與憂鬱。

一般而言，安養院與醫院是實施動物治療計畫的常見場所，因為老年人或病人在這些地方往往會感到寂寞。治療用動物的來訪通常一週安排一兩次，院友一般都很期待這些動物的來訪，這通常是他們當週最精彩的部分。有些醫院也有這樣的計畫，安排動物陪伴長期或末期病患一段時間。老人與病人因為接觸治療用動物而受益，讓他們覺得身體更健康、更有希望、更不寂寞。

不過，參與計畫的動物通常不是治療寵物組織所擁有的。擁有這些特殊動物的人通常是想要幫助老人與病人的義工。寵物成為這些計畫的一部分之前，必須先接受特定組織的評估。如果發現這些寵物合適，就會正式授權牠們加入動物治療計畫。

1. 本文的主旨為何？
(A) 治療用動物可以幫助病人和老人覺得更健康、更不寂寞。
(B) 大多數安養院和醫院都有動物治療計畫。

(C) 除了貓和狗，兔子和鳥類可也用來當治療用動物。
(D) 越來越多機構成立來訓練治療用動物。
全文主要說明治療用動物對病人和老人的幫助。

2. 下列何者不是好的治療用動物需要的特質？
(A) 友善的。　　　(B) 有耐性的。
(C) 情緒化的。　　(D) 溫馴的。
見第一段第三、四句。

3. 第二段 "short interactions" 指的是 _____。
(A) 聊天或觸摸　　(B) 輕撫或觸摸
(C) 凝視或輕撫　　(D) 拜訪或看護
線索在其上一段最後四個字。

4. 從本文可以類推出 _____。
(A) 狗是最好的治療用動物
(B) 治療用寵物成功與否取決於他們的主人
(C) 寵物帶給精神疾病者最大的好處
(D) 治療用寵物是期盼和希望的來源
線索在第三段第二句中的期待拜訪，以及同段最後一句的覺得更有希望。

5. 依據本文，下列何者為真？
(A) 行為不佳但友善的寵物在治療計畫中是受歡迎的。
(B) 住在安養院的人和醫院病人每天都有治療用寵物來訪。
(C) 治療用寵物在參與動物治療計畫之前都要接受評估。
(D) 治療計畫中使用的寵物都歸機構所有。
見最後一段第三句。

therapy　n.　治療	trait　n.　特質	stable　adj.　穩定的
interaction　n.　互動	resident　n.　居民	highlight　n.　最精彩部分
terminally　adv.　末期地	evaluate　v.　評估	authorization　n.　授權

16 全素主義的食物與理念
The Food and Philosophy of Veganism

人吃全素有很多種原因。有些人是因為關切食用動物的道德問題，有些人則是因為擔心健康。在道德方面，食用動物遭到虐待眾所皆知。有時候化妝品與肥皂也會以動物進行測試。此外，還有需要大量天然資源來飼養食用動物的議題。如果人類只種植與食用水果、蔬菜與穀物，對環境會比較好。

在健康方面，注重健康的全素者知道，食用天然蔬果、堅果、與全穀類對他們的健康很好。他們指出，不吃動物製品讓他們覺得自己更有活力與力氣。有些科學研究證實這種說法，顯示食用大量肉類並不健康，因為大型農場飼養食用動物時所用的一切人工藥劑使然。

吃全素本身可能會不健康嗎？畢竟，不吃任何動物製品難道不會危險嗎？不一定。仔細規劃的全素飲食可以提供身體所需的一切營養。吃全素的潛在問題包括無法攝取足夠的鐵與鈣，這些一般是從肉類與乳製品中獲得的。不過，食用大量的穀類、豆類與綠色蔬菜，一定可以獲得這些重要的營養素。此外，由於多數人由肉類攝取蛋白質，全素者必須特別小心，確定自己攝取足夠的蛋白質。非肉類蛋白質的不錯來源包括堅果、花生醬、豆腐、豆漿、與燕麥。

1. 本文未提到哪一項全素主義的理由？
(A) 健康。　　　　(B) 動物權利。
(C) 宗教。　　　(D) 環境。
第一段第二句和倒數兩句。

2. 那一類是全素食者不吃或不用的？
(A) 穀物。　　　　(B) 蔬菜。
(C) 皮革。　　　(D) 大豆。

線索在第一段文意及最後一句。

3. 第三段 "these important nutrients" 指的是 ＿＿＿。
(A) 蛋白質和鈣
(B) 鐵和鈣
(C) 鐵和鋅
(D) 蛋白質和鐵
線索在第三段第五句。

4. 依據本文，有時候全素食者不使用某些化妝品或肥皂是因為 ＿＿＿。
(A) 他們用動物來測試
(B) 他們取自於動物性產品
(C) 他們污染環境
(D) 他們引起皮膚過敏
見第一段第四句。

5. 本文的主要目的是 ＿＿＿。
(A) 比較　　　　(B) 娛樂
(C) 批評　　　　**(D) 提供知識**
本文主要提供有關全素主義的理由與知識。

veganism　n.　全素主義	ethics　n.　道德	cosmetics　n.　化妝品
issue　n.　議題	nutrient　n.　營養	potential　adj.　潛在的
calcium　n.　鈣	protein　n.　蛋白質	ensure　v.　確保

住在海平面下
Living Below Sea Level

紐奧良位於龐洽特雷恩湖 (Pontchartrain) 與鄰近墨西哥灣的密西西比河之間，一度曾是繁華的美國城市，以嘉年華會及傑出的爵士樂手著稱。在 2005 年卡崔娜 (Katrina) 颶風淹沒城市以前，有近乎五十萬人享受著該城市的悠閒文化。

紐奧良位於海平面以下兩米，形成一個碗狀，1960 年代興建的堤防系統防止周圍的水湧入。這些堤防或稱水堤，圍繞著整個城市，防止龐洽特雷恩湖與密西西比河的水湧入城市。有些堤防是混凝土製的，但很多都是土製的，環繞城市長達 210 公里。堤防內有抽水站及渠道，以便維持土地乾燥，即使大雨過後也一樣。

2005 年，卡崔娜颶風大舉重創紐奧良。卡崔娜的狂風暴雨摧毀了一些堤防。結果有八成以上的城市因此完全淹沒在水中，造成 1500 多人身亡，成千上萬人無家可歸，數千人斷糧、斷水或斷電。更慘的是，進出城市的主要道路都遭到摧毀或浸在水中，讓生還者很難離開城市，救援人員也難以進入。

聯邦與當地政府為了幫助這些人與他們的城市，已經花了數千億美元清理，搭蓋更好的堤防，重建受創家園與事業。不過，由於毀損程度太嚴重，有些專家估計，要讓城市復原並讓全部的人口返回，可能需要十年以上。

1. 下例何者不是紐奧良賴以防止淹水的措施？
   (A) 堤防。　　　　(B) 抽水站。
   (C) 渠道。　　　　**(D) 水壩。**
   見第二段第二句和第四句。

2. 卡崔娜颶風襲擊紐奧良之前，堤防系統運作良好，維持了大約 _____。

   (A) **45 年**　　　　(B) 65 年
   (C) 85 年　　　　(D) 100 年
   見第一段最後一句和第二段第一句。

3. 紐奧良形成碗狀位於海平面之下，被 _____ 圍繞著。
   (A) 密西西比河和墨西哥灣
   (B) 密西西比河和龐洽特雷恩湖
   (C) 墨西哥灣和龐洽特雷恩湖
   (D) 龐洽特雷恩湖和大西洋
   見第一段第一句。

4. 紐奧良以前的人口大約有 _____。
   (A) 30 萬人　　　　(B) 40 萬人
   (C) 50 萬人　　　　(D) 100 萬
   見第一段第二句。

5. 依據本文，以下何者為真？
   (A) 卡崔娜颶風使得整個城市都浸在水裡。
   (B) 卡崔娜颶風使數百名居民死亡。
   (C) 修復卡崔娜颶風造成的損害要花掉五年的時間。
   (D) 都市嚴重毀損，要進入救助難民非常困難。
   見第三段最後一句。

gulf	n.	海灣	thriving	adj.	繁榮的	levee	n.	堤防
concrete	n.	混凝土	surge	n.	(…的)激增	survivor	n.	生還者
federal	adj.	聯邦的	extent	n.	程度			

魔鬼氈：神奇黏扣帶
Velcro: the Wonder Fastener

粘扣帶又稱魔鬼氈，是一種非常重要的發明，在多數人的生活中扮演一大要角。這些粘扣帶用來接連不同的材質，例如布、塑膠、皮革等等。這項發明的點子實際上是來自於大自然。

第一條粘扣帶是由喬治・德・麥斯楚 (George de Mestral) 發明的，他是一位積極的自然觀察家。他看到多刺的種子囊黏附在他的羊毛衣與狗毛上。他不知道這些芒刺為什麼會緊附在他的衣服上，就用顯微鏡觀察它們，發現它們有很多小鉤子，可以黏住衣物的羊毛纖維。這促使他嘗試創造可以當粘扣帶的類似材質。

他認為他可以運用和天然芒刺一樣的原理製作粘扣帶：用一連串的鉤子緊緊抓住多毛的纖維層。於是他和很多織品製造商合作，成功地以棉質製作出第一個粘扣帶。他的粘扣帶分成兩部分：一邊有許多小鉤子，另一邊有平順的毛狀纖維。兩邊接在一起時，毛狀纖維會緊緊被鉤子抓住，讓兩者緊密相接。即使最初的粘扣帶對各種用途來說並不夠黏，但是以多種不同的材質製造便改善了粘扣帶的品質。

Velcro 這個名字是源於天鵝絨 (Velour) 與鉤子 (Crochet) 的法文字。這個名字後來和粘扣帶有關，因為麥斯楚把它的公司命名為 Velcro。不管是什麼名字，如今魔鬼氈因為強韌與方便，是大家認為不可或缺的必需品。

1. 本文的主旨為何？
   (A) 大自然被視為是最佳的發明者。
   (B) 喬治・德・麥斯楚喜愛兩件事：發明和戶外。
   (C) **魔鬼氈是由喬治・德・麥斯楚從大自然取得點子而發明的。**
   (D) 現今魔鬼氈這個神奇的粘扣帶應用在各個方面。
   全文主要談麥斯楚如何產生靈感發明魔鬼氈。

2. 第二段 "they" 這個代名詞指涉 ＿＿＿ 。
   (A) 衣服　　　　　(B) 纖維
   (C) 拜訪　　　　　**(D) 芒刺**

3. 第二段 "adhere" 這個字最適合以 ＿＿＿ 替代。
   (A) 觀察　　　　　**(B) 附著**
   (C) 改善　　　　　(D) 使繞成環
   線索在第二段第二句 attached 這個字。

4. 麥斯楚最初的粘扣帶是由什麼做成的？
   (A) 動物皮毛。　　**(B) 棉。**
   (C) 皮革。　　　　(D) 塑膠。
   見第三段第二句。

5. 依據本文，下列何者不實？
   (A) 麥斯楚把他魔鬼氈這個發明以兩個法文字命名。
   (B) 魔鬼氈實際上是麥斯楚的粘扣帶公司名。
   (C) **麥斯楚獨自工作終於做成了第一個粘扣帶。**
   (D) 經過許多改進，粘扣帶終於夠強韌足以黏著各種物體。
   見第三段第二句。

loop　n.　環	thorny　adj.　帶刺的	sac　n.　囊
adhere　v.　黏附	fiber　n.　纖維	layer　n.　層
fuzzy　adj.　多絨毛的	textile　n.　紡織品	velvet　n.　天鵝絨

長毛象是類似象的絕種動物,有捲長的象牙,披著又長又密的毛髮。牠們住在世界的北方,例如歐洲與北美等地。

woolly 意指「多毛的」。Mammoth 源自韃靼語,意指「土地」,因為幾世紀前發現長毛象的人以為這種生物活在地底下。雖然如今英語中這個字有「很大」的意思,但長毛象實際上並不大。牠們重 6 到 8 噸,最高 4 米。

這種絕種動物有什麼特別?與其他遠古動物相比,很多長毛象的化石與遺骸都找到了。再者,沒有其他遠古動物,例如恐龍,曾被發現是冰凍的。有 39 具冰凍的長毛象遺骸已經找到了,但只有 4 具是完整的。這些冰凍的遺骸正適合科學家做 DNA 測試,以便更深入了解牠們。

兩萬六千多年前,約有 100 隻長毛象困死在靠近現在南達科他州溫泉市西南角的池子裡。牠們是 1974 年時偶然被發現的。如今長毛象穴是世界上發現的最大長毛象遺骨集中地。遊客可以實際進入大型乾枯的窪地,觀賞和發現時維持一樣的骨骸。

科學家研究長毛象所得到的資訊,對於了解大象遺傳學來說很有價值。此外,他們可以更清楚幾千年前地球的樣子,了解什麼天候變化導致長毛象絕種。

1. 下列何者不是長毛象特別之處?
　(A) 沒有其他遠古動物被發現時是冰凍的。
　(B) 長毛象是最高的絕種動物。
　(C) 科學家可以將冰凍的長毛象作 DNA 測試。
　(D) 發現的長毛象遺骸比其他絕種動物還多。

見第二段第三句。

2. 科學家研究長毛象無法得知 ＿＿＿ 。
　(A) 長毛象絕種的原因
　(B) 大象的遺傳學
　(C) 地球幾世紀前的狀況
　(D) "mammoth" 這個字的真正意思
　見最後一段。

3. 長毛象不居住在 ＿＿＿ 。
　(A) 北美洲　　　　(B) 加拿大北部
　(C) 紐西蘭　　　(D) 歐洲
　見第一段第二句,紐西蘭在南半球。

4. 下列何者對長毛象穴的敘述不正確?
　(A) 遊客可以進入大的洞裡去看骸骨。
　(B) 長毛象的骨頭展示在櫥窗裡。
　(C) 這些長毛象死亡時間超過兩萬六千年。
　(D) 這些骸骨是無意中被發現的。
　見第四段第四句。

5. mammoth 在韃靼語中意思是土地,因為長久以來的想法是 ＿＿＿ 。
　(A) 長毛象曾在地上四處走動
　(B) 長毛象吃泥土
　(C) 長毛象是地球上最古老的物種
　(D) 長毛象住在地下
　見第二段第二句。

mammoth　n.　長毛象	extinct　adj.　絕種的	curved　adj.　彎曲的
tusk　n.　象牙	dense　adj.　濃密的	fossil　n.　化石
frozen　adj.　冰凍的	skeleton　n.　骨骸	genetics　n.　遺傳學

這是法利斯・哈珊(Farris Hassan)的故事：2005 年 12 月，他決定為高中的新聞學課程寫一篇報導，撰文者對於自己的報導必須有親身的經歷。哈珊想記錄伊拉克戰爭如何影響伊拉克人民。所以他在未告知任何人之下，就買了一張機票，飛往中東。

當這位大膽青年的故事傳到媒體時，全世界都報導了法利斯・哈珊令人難以置信的探險。記者們報導他最後如何抵達伊拉克，在旅途中如何遭遇麻煩。他雖然看起來像伊拉克人，卻不會說阿拉伯語。媒體與世界都把法利斯・哈珊捧為英雄。

很多人對於一位普通的青少年有膽子自己踏上這麼危險的旅程都感到驚訝。當媒體持續稱讚哈珊的冒險時，有些記者認為這個故事似乎「好得離譜」，便開始調查哈珊與他的伊拉克之旅。

記者發現法利斯・哈珊來自富裕的家庭。他們也獲悉他的雙親都是醫生，他念私立高中。媒體也發現法利斯從未修過新聞學課程，他的學校甚至沒開這門課。更糟的是，他的父親顯然在他出發以前就知道那次旅行，還幫他安排機票和旅遊簽證。

現在很多媒體認為哈珊的旅行只是男學生的惡作劇而已。但是為什麼有人會大費周章做這種事呢？很難想像法利斯除了後半輩子變成眾所皆知的說謊者外，他到底想獲得什麼。

1. 哈珊伊拉克之行的藉口是他要 _____。
   (A) 拜訪父母的朋友
   (B) 更瞭解伊拉克戰爭
   (C) 實際完成新聞學的課程
   (D) 揭發美國軍隊在伊拉克的作為
   見第一段第一句。

2. 為什麼有些記者決定調查哈珊和他的伊拉克之行？
   (A) 因為他有特別的家庭背景。
   (B) 因為他沒有這項學校功課。
   (C) 因為他不會說阿拉伯語。
   (D) 因為這故事太完美了。
   見第三段第二句。

3. 哈珊能夠獨自離家又安全地抵達伊拉克是 _____ 的幫忙。
   (A) 他母親　　　　**(B) 他父親**
   (C) 他的校長　　　(D) 一些記者
   見第四段最後一句。

4. 哈珊的故事很快引起媒體注意是因為 _____。
   (A) 他們佩服這個青少年獨自旅行的勇氣
   (B) 他們很驚訝他說話的方式
   (C) 他們很驚訝這個青少年對伊拉克人民的態度
   (D) 他們好奇他對伊拉克戰爭的看法
   見第三段第一句。

5. 第二段 "hailed" 這個字最適合以 _____ 替代。
   (A) 叫喊　　　　　(B) 連結
   (C) 認可　　　　(D) 鄙視
   線索是 hail 之後的幾個字，尤其是 as。

bogus	adj.	假的	journalism	n.	新聞學

journalist　n.　記者
hail　v.　讚揚　　　guts　n.　勇氣　　　investigate　v.　調查
enroll　v.　註冊修課　visa　n.　簽證　　　prank　n.　惡作劇

21 伊娃‧裴隆
Eva Peron

1919 年，伊娃‧裴隆 (Eva Peron) 生於阿根廷的洛斯托鐸斯 (Los Toldos) 小鎮上。身為農場主人與情婦所生的女兒，伊娃在不公平、不穩定與貧困的陰影之下成長。她 7 歲時，父親過世。她和家人必須為富有的家庭烹飪維生。年輕貌美的伊娃夢想逃離困境。

伊娃年僅 15 歲時，就逃家前往阿根廷的首都布宜諾斯艾利斯 (Buenos Aires)。她在那裡碰到幾位有權勢的追求者，幫她在廣播肥皂劇及電影中找到演出工作。她靠著和這些人一連串的風花雪月，終於逐步嶄露頭角。伊娃成功了，卻不是她真正想要的名聲，所以她決定將她的野心朝向政治圈。她 25 歲時，開始和軍官胡安‧裴隆 (Juan Peron) 交往。這對野心勃勃的佳偶是天作之合，很快就在 1945 年結婚了。

次年，胡安當選總統，伊娃變成第一夫人，是阿根廷最有權力的女性。但是她並未忘記自己的身世背景，並運用她的影響力建造醫院、學校與窮人和老人的居所。因此，伊娃極受一般人民的愛戴。不過，她有很多敵人。上流社會嫉妒她崇高的社會地位，指控她是利用男人「陪睡出頭」。伊娃不尊重反對者的人權，也因此顯露出她人格的黑暗面。她讓很多人入獄，也支持先生加強運用軍權掌控國家。

1951 年，悲劇突然發生。伊娃罹患癌症，隔年年僅 33 歲便撒手西歸。不過，伊娃‧裴隆已經達成她的人生目標——她已經成為、也一直是阿根廷史上最出名的女性。

1. 伊娃人生第一次享有成功是當 _____。
　(A) 廚師　　　　　　(B) **演員**
　(C) 社會工作者　　　(D) 捍衛人權者

見第二段第二、三句。

2. 第二段 "them" 這個代名詞指涉 _____。
　(A) 工作　　　　　　(B) 電影
　(C) **追求者**　　　　(D) 新聞界

3. 寫本文的目的是 _____。
　(A) **提供伊娃‧裴隆的簡要自傳**
　(B) 顯示伊娃如何利用權力
　(C) 描述伊娃如何捍衛人權
　(D) 說明伊娃為何進入政治圈
　全文敘述她的一生。

4. 依據本文下列何者為真？
　(A) 伊娃在阿根廷人民眼中是惡魔。
　(B) **伊娃對待她的反對者不公且殘酷。**
　(C) 伊娃童年過得很快樂。
　(D) 伊娃 1951 年死於癌症。
　見第三段倒數兩句，(D) 選項應該改為 1952 年。

5. 伊娃被阿根廷人民愛戴是因為 _____。
　(A) 她是一個迷人又複雜的女人
　(B) 她來自貧困地區
　(C) **她致力於幫助窮人和老人**
　(D) 她是這國家最有權勢男人的妻子
　見第三段第二、三句。

mistress　n.　情婦	uncertainty　n.　不穩定	prosperity　n.　成功；繁榮
accuse　v.　指控	opponent　n.　對手	imprison　v.　監禁

22 等等！我從未買過那個東西！
Wait a Minute! I Never Bought That!

試想有一天，你接到電器行打來的憤怒電話，要你為一台昂貴的冰箱支付數千元的帳單。問題是，你根本沒向那家店買過任何東西！很顯然地，你已經淪為身份竊盜的受害者，而身份竊盜是全世界成長最快的罪行。當竊賊偷取你的個人資訊並偽裝成你時，就構成身份竊盜，他們這麼做通常是為了購買昂貴的東西或犯下其他形式的詐騙。身份竊盜往往隱於無形，它所引起的傷害可能需要好幾年才能彌補。

身份竊盜迅速散播的原因有很多。第一，大家抗拒可以讓信用卡更安全的法律。他們貪圖方便遠重於安全。第二，上網購物的逐漸風行衍生出新的風險。竊賊可以透過假網頁、電子郵件、以及其他詭計輕鬆竊取你的資訊。稍後他們可以再上網登入匿名購物，不必冒險親自盜刷偽卡。第三，拜網路與手機之賜，身份竊盜者可以向不同國家的人竊取個人資訊，讓他們幾乎無法被找到並加以逮捕。

好消息是有幾種簡單的方法可以保護你自己。如果你接到來自銀行或公司的詭異電話向你詢問資訊，就掛斷電話。然後查出該公司公佈的電話或網頁，並要求和客服部門談話。那樣就可以確定和你說話的人不是騙子。另外，文件丟棄以前一定要撕碎。最後，不要忘記檢查你的信用卡帳單，有任何可疑收費便立即舉報。

1. 身份盜竊發生在 ＿＿＿＿ 的時候。
　(A) 小偷闖進屋裡偷走個人資料
　(B) 小偷偷竊並盜用某人的個人資料去犯罪
　(C) 有人試圖進入電腦系統以散佈病毒
　(D) 有人經由網路威脅別人

見第一段第四句。

2. 本文中哪個字和 "fraud" 字義最接近？
　(A) 方便。　　　　　(B) 費用。
　(C) 普遍。　　　　　**(D) 欺騙。**
　線索在這個字前面的 commit other forms of，所以此字也會是犯罪的一種。

3. 作者提出「另外，文件丟棄以前一定要撕碎」這句話的目的為何？
　(A) 警告說小偷或許會從垃圾取得個人資料。
　(B) 提供一個收集垃圾的好方法。
　(C) 討論有關文件和垃圾的問題。
　(D) 說明為何文件很重要。
　由最後一段談如何保護自己可以推斷其目的。

4. 下列何者未在本文中敘述？
　(A) 罪犯可以從假網頁竊取資料。
　(B) 身份盜竊的問題世界各地都有。
　(C) 網路購物讓偷取有用資料變得更容易。
　(D) 罪犯會從信箱偷取銀行或信用卡帳單。

5. 第一段 "it" 這個代名詞指涉 ＿＿＿＿。
　(A) 個人資料　　　　(B) 損害
　(C) 身份盜竊　　　(D) 問題

victim　n.　受害者	identity　n.　身份	theft　n.　竊盜
fraud　n.　詐騙	invisible　adj.　看不見的	anonymously　adv.　匿名地
shred　v.　撕碎	document　n.　文件	suspicious　adj.　可疑的

23 動物警報
Animal Alerts

　　1975 年，中國海城市發生 7.3 級的地震。地震發生前幾天，市府官員已下令撤離。這是接獲當地居民通報蛇從冬眠中竄出，凍死在路上後所做的決定。如果市民全在，地震可能會造成十萬人喪生。2004 年，有人看見寇立 (Khao Lak) 有兩隻受驚嚇的大象，在該地被大海嘯摧毀前 5 分鐘掙脫鎖鍊並逃向高地。不解的人跟隨其後而保住性命。

　　人類發現動物在天災之前會做出一些恐慌與奇特的事。例如，狗會不斷地嗥叫。豬會開始互咬。蜜蜂會突然飛離蜂窩。老鼠會暈眩地四處走動，很容易徒手捕捉，而幸運的是貓也都躲起來了。

　　野生動物專家認為，動物比人類更有能力察覺周遭的變化。他們敏銳的聽覺和人類的很不一樣。海嘯可能引發聲波，透過海底岩石構造傳送的速度比水面上還快。大象可以先聽到聲波，並且有時間逃離。研究人員也指出，很多動物可以感受到地震之前的震波或空氣中電流的改變。

　　即使我們無法實際證明動物可以感應天災，卻很難忽略牠們的預警能力。所以當信鴿迷路或魚兒開始跳出水面時，就要提高警覺了。如果我們無法像動物一樣機警，我們至少應該觀察他們！

1. 下列哪一項可能是市府官員在地震發生前給海城居民的訊息？
   (A) 躲起來，否則他們會找到你。
   (B) 整理乾淨，否則會生病。
   (C) 當心，否則會受傷。
   (D) 搬走，否則會死。

線索在第一段第四句的假設，和第二句的 **evacuation** (撤離)。

2. 研究人員認為下列那哪一項是動物可以預測地震的理由？
   (A) 動物能看見地震對地面造成的改變。
   (B) 動物能聽到建築物塌造成的聲波。
   (C) 動物能感覺到地面的震動或空氣中電流的改變。
   (D) 動物能聞到地震的震波。

見第三段最後一句。

3. 下列哪一項最可以描述作者對於把動物當作天然災害偵測器的態度？
   (A) 大多數科學家不同意動物行為可以用來預測天然災害的想法。
   (B) 動物靠警覺生存，人應該從他們身上找線索。
   (C) 一直都沒有證據顯示動物有能力感知地震。
   (D) 動物雖然感官敏銳，但經常死於天然災害。

最後一段作者提出他的看法。

4. 第三段 "them" 這個代名詞指涉 _____。
   (A) 岩層　　　　　　**(B) 聲波**
   (C) 人類　　　　　　(D) 環境

them 之前的 **hear** 為本題線索。

5. 在這次海城地震發生之前，人們發現哪一項特別的動物行為？
   (A) 蛇從冬眠中爬出來。
   (B) 狗不停嗥叫。
   (C) 魚從水中跳出來。
   (D) 蜜蜂飛離蜂窩。

見第一段第三句。

---

magnitude　n.　震級　　　　evacuation　n.　撤離　　　　hibernation　n.　冬眠

tsunami　n.　海嘯　　　　　howl　v.　嗥叫　　　　　　seismic　adj.　地震的

24 *垃圾郵件的問題*
The Problems with Spam

你覺得你收到太多的電子郵件廣告嗎？這些不需要的電子訊息通常稱為「垃圾郵件」，佔了全世界郵件總收發量的一半。每年公司為了擺脫這些訊息，需要耗費數十億美元，因為他們的員工會浪費寶貴的時間刪除訊息。代價更大的是，公司還必須在軟體上耗費數百萬美元，在垃圾訊息寄抵達公司電腦之前就先掌握與過濾它們。

垃圾郵件不僅浪費時間與金錢，也可能是有害的。有些垃圾訊息內藏「間諜軟體」，亦即一種可以從電腦中取得秘密或個人資料的電腦軟體。其他的垃圾郵件可能內含「病毒」，這也是一種隱藏軟體程式，可以使用他人的電子郵件寄送垃圾郵件、或是提供資訊給竊賊或駭客，幫他們找到入侵電腦的辦法。有些電腦病毒會乾脆刪除電腦內的一切，讓電腦毫無用武之地並毀損重要的資訊。

不幸的是，並沒多少方法可以減少垃圾郵件的發送。阻擋垃圾郵件的軟體開發時，發送垃圾郵件的人就會想辦法躲避障礙。政府似乎也無力控管垃圾郵件，因為網路是國際性的，一國的反垃圾郵件法令不一定適用於其他國家。而且每次有發送垃圾郵件的人被捕時，似乎都另有他人遞補其位子。

即便垃圾郵件是嚴重的問題，還是有方法保護自己和你的電腦。如果你不認識寄件人，絕對不要開啟電子郵件的附件。不要在網頁上公開你的電子郵件地址。只向你認識的人透露你的主要電子郵件地址。

1. 以下何者最能描述垃圾郵件？
(A) 垃圾郵件包含電子郵件訊息。
(B) 垃圾郵件是一種電子郵件軟體。
(C) 垃圾郵件是網路版的垃圾郵件。
(D) 垃圾郵件是免費的網頁電子郵件服務。
見第一段第二句。

2. 第二段主要是有關 _____。
(A) 間諜軟體的資料
(B) 網路駭客在做什麼
(C) 重要資料的遺失
(D) 垃圾郵件帶來的病毒和間諜軟體
見第二段第二、三句。

3. 本文未提到哪一項垃圾郵件無法大量減少的原因？
(A) 沒有反垃圾郵件軟體是百分之百有效的。
(B) 不可能逮捕所有發送垃圾郵件者。
(C) 發送垃圾郵件者總是從同行買到電子郵件地址。
(D) 垃圾郵件是世界性的問題；一國的反垃圾郵件法不一定適用他國。
見第三段。

4. 本文未提到哪一項避免垃圾郵件的方法？
(A) 設一個安全的電子郵件密碼。
(B) 不要在網路上公開你的電子郵件地址。
(C) 不要開啟來路不明的電子郵件附加檔案。
(D) 不要把你的主要電子郵件地址給不認識的人。
見最後一段。

5. 第一段 "filter" 這個字最適合以 _____ 替代。
(A) 保留 **(B) 除去** (C) 復原 (D) 恢復
線索是這個字之前的相關字 **catch**。

spam	n.	垃圾郵件	
hacker	n.	駭客	
delete	v.	刪除	
block	v.	阻擋	
filter	v.	過濾	
bypass	v.	避開	

　　如果你到明尼蘇達州 (Minnesota) 布魯明頓 (Bloomington) 的明尼亞波利斯 (Minneapolis) 郊區，你會看到一座巨大的購物中心「美國購物中心」。購物中心的運作就像小鎮一樣，雇用 11,000 多人在 520 幾家商店與 7 英畝的室內主題樂園內工作，夏天還有 2000 位臨時工來幫忙。另外，購物中心裡還有一個水族館、樂高想像中心、恐龍漫步館及電玩區。

　　但是，這些名稱都無法讓人實際了解美國購物中心到底有多大。為了比較，巨大的 4 層樓複合式建築裡可以裝下 32 台波音 747 飛機。如果一家店逛 10 分鐘，逛完全部需要花 86 個小時以上。

　　多數人造訪購物中心是為了到裡面許多有名的商店逛街，例如梅西百貨 (Macy's)、布魯明黛百貨 (Bloomingdale's) 或諾斯壯百貨 (Nordstrom)。其他訪客則是來目睹與體驗購物中心的 7 英畝室內主題樂園，內有兩座雲霄飛車及許多刺激的遊樂設施、遊戲與吸引人的事物。它每年吸引四千兩百萬名遊客。

　　如果所有的逛街與活動讓你感到飢腸轆轆，有很多地方可以用餐。至少有 26 家速食餐廳提供多元的食物，例如美國與亞洲食物，或是許多異國風味的冰淇淋。如果你想要更精緻的晚餐，可以試試許多專賣牛排或海鮮的正式餐廳。

　　明尼蘇達州的冬天雖然寒冷，但是由樂園上方高窗照進來的日光和照明系統讓購物中心維持舒適的溫度。購物中心內部一年到頭都使用空調保持空氣的清新與流通。不管是哪個季節，訪客體驗世界最大的購物中心時，都覺得相當舒服。

1. 這座個購物中心每年吸引多少訪客？
   (A) 兩千六百萬。
   (B) 三千兩百萬。
   (C) 四千兩百萬。
   (D) 八千六百萬。
   見第三段最後一句。

2. 美國購物中心位於 ＿＿＿＿＿。
   (A) 冬季天氣溫和的地區
   (B) 在明尼蘇達州的布魯明頓
   (C) 樂高想像中心附近
   (D) 布魯明黛百貨附近
   見第一段第一句。(A) 選項見第五段第一句。

3. 本文中哪個字和 "huge" 的字義最接近？
   (A) 優雅的。　　　　(B) 各種的。
   (C) 巨大的。　　　(D) 異國的。
   第一段第一句的 **enormous shopping mall** 和第二段第二句的 **huge complex** 是同義詞。

4. 依據本文，下列哪一項不實？
   (A) 這座購物中心有超過 520 間商店。
   (B) 空調系統終年運轉。
   (C) 上方裝有高窗好讓陽光照進來。
   (D) 這座購物中心有包含兩座雲霄飛車的戶外主題樂園。
   見第三段第二句。

5. 下列哪一項可以由本文類推出來？
   (A) 夏季遊客比其他三季多。
   (B) 大多數人為了主題樂園而來此購物中心。
   (C) 這座購物中心是全美最吸引遊客的景點。
   (D) 遊客們大多數來自其他國家。
   由第一段第二句夏季時需要額外的 **2000** 名幫手可以得知。

---

aquarium　n.　水族館	high profile　adj.　引人注目的	roller coaster　雲霄飛車
annually　adv.　每年地	exotic　adj.　異國的	circulate　v.　使流通

26 追風者
Storm Chasers

在美國，尤其是平坦空曠的草原州，龍捲風非常普遍。在龍捲風季節期間，好幾百位不支薪的娛樂追風者湧入常發生龍捲風的州，攜帶著追蹤龍捲風的高科技裝備。有些人有特別的車子，配有追蹤器與偵測器、攝影機、強化玻璃、電話和防滾架。這些設備讓車子碰上真正的龍捲風時不易被摧毀。多數的追風者會跟著龍捲風跑，以便捕捉精彩的照片或影像片段。

雖然多數的追風者偏好與龍捲風的預期路徑保持一點距離，有些人卻喜歡捲入暴風中的刺激。這些人是追求刺激者。他們使用和娛樂追風者一樣的昂貴設備，密切鎖定龍捲風位置的即時報導，以便盡可能地靠近龍捲風。他們讓自己身陷極大的險境，希望拍到完美的照片或幾分鐘的影片，以便賣給電視台、月曆出版商及報社。

還有另一群追風者的工作是擔任導遊，帶領有興趣的人。這些有支薪的導遊在遠處尾隨著龍捲風，不過度冒上生命危險，但依舊可以為人們帶來追風的刺激感。導遊通常會告訴顧客很多有趣的訊息，同時保護他們的安全，避免龍捲風刮起的強風、閃電與飛屑等。

很多追風者認為追逐龍捲風並沒有非常危險，但是每年有很多人因為意外狂風而喪命卻是不爭的事實。所以除非你受過適當的安全訓練，否則千萬別嘗試追逐龍捲風。

1. 本文提到幾種追逐龍捲風的人？
  (A) 兩種。　　　　(B) **三種。**
  (C) 四種。　　　　(D) 五種。
  見第一段第二句、第二段第二句和第三段第一句。

2. 龍捲風位置的即時報導有助於尋求刺激者 _____ 。
  (A) **盡可能接近龍捲風**
  (B) 知道龍捲風有多強烈
  (C) 陷入極大的危險
  (D) 被地方性報紙報導出來
  見第二段第三句。

3. 尋求刺激者 _____ 。
  (A) 想要以精良設備工作得到娛樂
  (B) 想要靠近龍捲風的刺激並得到錢
  (C) **享受追逐的刺激並得到精彩的照片和影像**
  (D) 想要賣照片或影像並提供「追風旅遊」的服務
  見第二段第三、四句。

4. 依據本文，下列何者有關「追風旅遊」領隊的敘述是不正確的？
  (A) 他們保護顧客不受龍捲風傷害。
  (B) 他們教導顧客許多有關龍捲風的知識。
  (C) 他們跟龍捲風保持安全距離。
  (D) **他們提供免費的旅遊服務。**
  見第三段第二句。

5. 最後一段 "claim" 最適合以 _____ 替代。
  (A) 冒險　(B) 給　**(C) 取**　(D) 引導
  claim 之後的 lives 是線索，take lives 指「奪取性命」。

prairie　n.　大草原	tornado　n.　龍捲風	footage　n.　影像片段
thrill　n.　刺激	coverage　n.　新聞報導	debris　n.　碎片，殘骸

由於單身男女往往太忙，以致於無法透過傳統交友方式相見，如今很多人上網尋找戀情。這種作法稱為網路交友。其中一種網路交友的形式是到網路的聊天室聊天。如果兩人在聊天室立刻就很契合，就可以向對方傳送即時訊息，以便私下聊天。

另一種網路交友形式則是牽涉到個人網站，例如 Match.com 或 Eharmony.com。在這些網站上，男女生可以貼出內含資訊與照片的簡介。然後他們可以瀏覽其他單身者的簡介，用電子郵件聯絡他們感興趣的人。

可惜的是，網路上騙取他人錢財的「詐騙者」充斥。根據美國聯邦調查局的資料顯示，光是 2006 年就有超過二十萬的美國人因為網路詐騙而損失近乎兩億美元。這些詐騙案中有 12 % 是始於即時通訊，2.4 % 是來自於聊天室。而且，還有無數上個人網站尋找伴侶卻找到騙子的故事。或許最慘的例子是一位女人給一位男人十萬美元幫他打拼事業，後來才發現他已婚而且還退休了。

選擇網路交友的人應該遵循一些原則以求自保。他們應該避免回答太私密的問題，對於開口要錢的人要小心提防。更重要的是，如果決定親自見面，一定要在公開場合。

網路交友是現代尋找戀情的常見方法。對於有意識到危險並想辦法避免的人來說，網路交友可以是既安全又有效的。

1. 本文的主旨為何？
   (A) 網路使用者最好注意網路詐騙。
   (B) 網路交友是找到愛情安全又有效的的方法。
   (C) 網路交友變得普遍，但有潛在的危險。
   (D) 網路使人可以和世界各地的人往來。
   本文探討網路交友以及它可能有的危險。

2. 本文未提到以下哪一個網路所提供的網路交友環境？
   (A) 網路聊天室。　　(B) 新聞網頁。
   (C) 即時訊息服務。 (D) 個人網站

3. 第一段 "hit it off" 這個片語的意思很可能是 ＿＿＿ 。
   (A) 喜歡彼此競爭
   (B) 與他人意見不合
   (C) 立刻喜歡上彼此
   (D) 面臨相同的問題
   由本句文意可猜出此片語的意思。

4. 下列何者被認為是第三段所稱的「騙子」？
   (A) 使用假網頁盜取身份的人。
   (B) 用電話和 ATM 盜取金融資料的人。
   (C) 用假電子郵件盜取銀行帳戶和密碼的人。
   (D) 假裝尋找網路戀情卻欺騙感情又詐騙錢財的人。
   線索就在下一句。

5. 文中未提到哪一項網路交友安全的建議？
   (A) 要在公共場所見面。
   (B) 不要提供你自己的個人資料。
   (C) 如果有人要求財物上的幫忙，一定小心。
   (D) 有機會見面的時候，帶著朋友一起去。
   見第四段。

instant message	v. 以即時訊息聯絡	personals website	個人網站
via	prep. 經由	scam	n. 詐騙

browse　v. 瀏覽
adopt　v. 採取

「綠色建築」就是建造對環境影響有限的環保建築。這些建築比一般建築使用較少的能源在冷暖氣及照明上,而且通常建在四周環繞當地土生植物的地區。

綠色建築的建造嘗試採用附近即可取得的材料。外部建材很少或不會使用,所以只需運送少數材料到當地,也因此運輸時需要的化石燃料的使用被控制到最低。

綠色建築的案例之一是在明尼蘇達州的羅傑斯(Rogers)。羅傑斯高中首先建在既有的道路附近,以把對環境的破壞減少到最低。建築的設計可以有效運用自然的光線,所以白天不需要燈光。他們不從建築物之外打進空氣,而是搭建通風系統,讓空氣在整個建築中清新地流通,而不用外部電力資源。

在德國的弗萊堡(Freiburg)可以看到其他綠色建築的例子。這些建築是住家,使用很少的電力在冬天取暖、在夏天保持涼爽。他們藉由很棒的隔離與通風系統以做到這些。屋頂有太陽能板可以發電,而它們實際上發的電比居民需要的還多。

對活在全球暖化時代的我們來說,綠色建築可能是解決問題的部分解答,因為它們降低產生的廢料量,並使用乾淨的能源。不過,它們還不是很普遍。為了拯救我們的地球,綠色建築最後可能會變成未來的標準。

1. 依據本文,使用「綠色建築」的主要目的是 _____ 。
   (A) 降低建築費用　(B) 減低對環境的衝擊
   (C) 改善公共衛生　(D) 減低維修費用
   見第一段第一句。

2. 下列哪一項可能未曾被羅傑斯高中的設計師考慮過?
   (A) 建築地點。　　(B) 電力資源的減少。
   (C) 回收的建材。　(D) 自然光。
   見第三段。

3. 在德國弗萊堡的綠色建築有好的隔離和通風系統是為了減少 _____ 的能源。
   (A) 暖氣和照明　　(B) 暖氣和冷氣
   (C) 冷氣和排水　　(D) 烹飪和照明
   見第四段第二句。

4. 依據本文,下列何者為真?
   (A) 綠色建築不需要綠葉植物。
   (B) 綠色建築很容易在世界各地見到。
   (C) 在弗萊堡的綠色建築由太陽能板發電。
   (D) 羅傑斯高中用空調系統把新鮮空氣送入建築物中。
   見第四段第四句。

5. 盡量使用當地建材建造綠色建築的目的是 _____ 。
   (A) 幫助地方產業興盛
   (B) 為將來訂定新標準
   (C) 將額外建材的需要減至最低
   (D) 減少使用在運輸上的能源
   見第二段第二句。

native	adj.	土生的	
insulation	n.	隔離,絕緣	
minimum	n.	最小值	
ventilation	n.	通風	
pump	v.	輸送	
norm	n.	標準	

在家教育或是傳統教育？
Homeschooling or a Traditional Education?

　　如今在家教育的情況逐漸增加。愈來愈多的家長選擇在自己家中提供子女教育。

　　這些家長為何選擇在家教育呢？有些人認為，子女在公立學校碰到太多的同儕壓力，讓他們更難培養良好的人格特質。其他家長則是對正規學校的教學課程感到不滿。他們想決定什麼對子女是重要而應該學習的，而不是放任政府官僚決定。此外，在家教育還可以讓子女用適合他們發展階段的方式學習，而且可以在適當時機介紹技能與概念。

　　在家教育的教學方式各不相同。有些家長依循嚴格的計畫表，仿效傳統學校的環境。其他家長採取最徹底的在家教育模式，不打分數或考試，讓小孩念他們想讀的東西。不過，多數的家長是採取中庸的方法，在自由與架構間取得平衡。

　　美國最近的研究顯示，在家教育的孩子和一般學生考 SAT (學術評量測驗) 的成績一樣高。此外，由於大學要找的是有獨特經驗的學生，在家教育的學生受大學錄取的成功率較高一些。在家教育的學生在英文與藝術之類的學科上通常表現較好，但是在數學與科學方面則稍微比較不熟練。

　　父母在決定是否在家教育子女時，有很多權衡需要考慮。在家教育可能所費不貲，而且至少必須有一位家長全職在家監督教育。此外，很多在家教育的學生覺得寂寞。他們可能想要成為校隊的一份子。在家教育也需要家長和子女都有高度的紀律。不過，一般認為在家教育的好處遠勝過缺點。

1. 作者對在家教育的態度如何？

(A) **贊成。** (B) 反對。 (C) 中立。 (D) 懷疑。
見本文最後一句。

2. 本文未提到下列哪一項造成在家教育人數增加的因素？
(A) 同儕壓力。　　(B) 教育成就。
(C) **安全考量。**　　(D) 教育課程。
見第二段第二、三、五句。

3. 下列哪一項有關在家教育是不正確的？
(A) 在家教育的孩子和一般孩子在 SAT 測驗的成績相當。
(B) 在家教育的學生申請大學比較容易被接受。
(C) 在家教育的孩子或許會與社會隔離。
(D) **在家教育的學生數學和科學得分較高。**
見第四段最後一句。

4. 第三段中 "a radical form of homeschooling" 提供孩子很多 ＿＿＿＿。
(A) 結構 (B) **自由** (C) 服務 (D) 計畫
線索在同一句的 in which 子句。

5. 可以由本文類推出 ＿＿＿＿。
(A) 在家教育的父母一般都比較學識淵博
(B) 只有父母能決定他們家是否適合在家教育
(C) **在家教育的過程中，父母和孩子或許會無法自我控制**
(D) 在家教育的孩子聰明、成熟、有創造力而且獨立
證據在最後一段的倒數第二句 discipline (紀律)。

trait n. 特質	bureaucracy n. 官僚	concept n. 概念
radical adj. 徹底的	admission n. 准許進入	trade off n. 權衡
supervise v. 監督	outweigh v. 勝過	drawback n. 缺點

30 奧比斯的故事
The ORBIS Story

1970 年代中期，在休士頓 (Houston) 執業的眼科醫師大衛·巴頓博士 (David Paton)，他看見開發中國家對於可醫治的眼疾無能為力，因而感到苦惱。他想出一個計畫，把科技與技術放進飛機裡，創造出「飛行眼科醫院」，可以飛往任何需要的地方。除了照顧開發中國家的病患外，巴頓博士的目的是要協助教育當地的醫師，讓他們可以繼續這個工作。

1982 年，在美國國際開發總署的財務補助與私人捐助下，奧比斯國際機構成立了。聯合航空捐贈一台退役的 DC-8 飛機，做為第一架「飛行眼科醫院」。在轉變成全功能的教學眼科醫院後，它便開始服務。1982 年，它飛到巴拿馬 (Panama) 進行第一次的訓練任務。從那時起，奧比斯便致力在開發中國家消弭不必要的失明及恢復人民的視力。

如今，奧比斯已經變成知名的國際非營利與非政府組織，提供免費的醫療與防治失明的訓練。奧比斯的成員都是義工，包括 400 多位醫學專業人士及 17 位為「飛行眼科醫院」駕駛的飛行員。如今的「飛行眼科醫院」是奧比斯在 1992 年以一千四百萬美元購買的 DC-10 飛機。它初次的開刀任務是 1994 年到中國北京。新的飛機上內建手術室、恢復室以及教室。

奧比斯也在很多國家裡實施醫院計畫，和當地的醫學組織合作防治失明及治療眼疾。據估計已有一百多萬人接受過奧比斯的治療，還有 80 幾國十二萬四千多位當地的保健專業人士已透過奧比斯計畫提升醫術。

1. 奧比斯國際機構的任務是 _____ 。
  (A) 為眼科醫師設立永久的政府計畫
  (B) 在已開發國家執行醫院計畫
  (C) 在開發中國家治療眼疾以及教育當地醫生
  (D) 為全世界的眼科醫生提供教育和訓練
  見第一段第二、三句。

2. 目前的「飛行眼科醫院」 _____ 。
  (A) 是一架聯合航空公司捐贈的 DC-8 飛機
  (B) 在 1992 年開始服勤
  (C) 是 1994 年由奧比斯購買的 DC-10 飛機
  (D) 包含一間手術室、一間恢復室和一間教室
  見第三段最後一句。

3. 第一段的代名詞 "it" 指涉 _____ 。
  (A) 技術   (B) 眼科醫師
  (C) 飛行眼科醫院   (D) 計畫

4. 第二段 "converted" 最適合以 _____ 替代。
  (A) 轉變 (B) 運輸 (C) 解散 (D) 遞送
  converted 之後的文意是線索。

5. 依據本文，下列何者為真？
  (A) 奧比斯國際機構在 1992 年設立。
  (B) 1970 年代大衛·巴頓博士有了成立奧比斯的構想。
  (C) 飛行眼科醫院第一次的訓練任務是去中國。
  (D) 這座移動醫院的飛行員並非義工。
  見第一段第一、二句。

ophthalmologist	n.	眼科醫師	grant	n.	認可
convert	v.	轉變	functional	adj.	功能的
eliminate	v.	消除	enhance	v.	提升

donation	n.	捐贈
strive	v.	致力於

31 尼斯湖水怪
The Monster of Loch Ness

在蘇格蘭高地 (Scottish Highlands) 有個美麗的湖泊名為尼斯湖。該湖以湖內居住者尼斯水怪著稱。

一千五百多年前，一位聖徒的傳記中首次出現水怪的記載。不過直到 1930 年，水怪才登上頭條，3 位漁夫表示看到水中騷動，有一條約莫 20 英尺長的巨型龍狀動物突然出現。雖然他們的船劇烈搖晃，但水怪並沒有傷害他們。這起事件發生以後，很多人都宣稱看到怪物，以湖名將它命名為「尼西」。大家知道水怪並沒有造成任何傷害，人們甚至認為看見水怪是個好兆頭。

沒人確知水怪的樣子。有些人說牠像是沒有爪子的長頸鱷魚。其他人把它形容成有紅色的嘴和突出的大角的巨型蛇狀動物。

1982 年，名叫羅伯・克雷格 (Robert Craig) 的蘇格蘭工程師發表最有可能的說法。他宣稱所謂的水怪，實際上是分布於該區域周邊、沒入水底的蘇格蘭松樹幹。這些樹幹長年沈在湖底，有時候會因為壓力差異而浮到水面。樹幹浮起時，會釋放出樹幹裡的氣體，使水中出現漣漪與泡沫。然後或許是最後一次，樹幹又再度下沈。

有些人認為沒有水怪這回事，覺得尼西只是虛構。但多數人拒絕相信這套理論，持續聚到湖邊窺探他們喜愛的尼斯湖水怪。

1. 尼斯湖水怪的名字來自 _____ 。
   (A) 最初報導它的人
   (B) 它居住的湖
   (C) 最初拍它的照片的人
   (D) 它居住的湖的形狀

見第二段倒數第二句。

2. 水怪的出現第一次被記載於 _____ 。
   (A) 1939 年　　　　(B) 1982 年
   (C) 6 世紀　　　 (D) 16 世紀
   見第二段第一句。

3. 下列有關 1930 年水怪出現的報導哪一項是不正確的？
   (A) 水怪被認為大約有 20 英尺長。
   (B) 水怪被認為是像魚類的大型動物。
   (C) 這次報導吸引大眾的注意。
   (D) 水怪並未對那 3 個漁夫造成傷害。
   見第二段第二句。

4. 第四段 "submerged" 這個字和 _____ 字義最接近。
   (A) 飄浮的　　　　(B) 浮現的
   (C) 已發展的　　　**(D) 水面下的**
   線索是下一句的 at the bottom of the loch。

5. 依據羅伯・克雷格的理論，下列何者為真？
   (A) 所謂的水怪只是橡樹的樹幹。
   (B) 水怪浮出水面呼吸。
   (C) 水怪看起來像鱷魚。
   (D) 壓力的差異造成所謂的水怪出現。
   見第四段第三句。

resident n. 居民	saint n. 聖徒	omen n. 預兆
alligator n. 鱷魚	submerged adj. 沒入水底的	ripple n. 漣漪
myth n. 虛構的事物	glimpse n. 一瞥	

32 第一張郵票
The First Postage Stamp

1840 年以前，英國還沒有郵票。郵資不是用手寫就是用墨水印在信封上。收件人必須支付運費，而非寄件人。郵差送件時要擔負起向不情願的收件人收取郵資的艱鉅任務。有時候因為郵資太貴，有人會拒絕收信。他們負擔不起郵務系統。

1837 年，羅蘭・希爾 (Rowland Hill) 在《郵局改革：重要性與實用性》中提出革新性的點子，統一以一便士的低郵資寄件到英國各地。他也建議寄件者應該支付郵資，而非收件者；郵資計價基礎應該由距離改成重量；還有應該藉由在信封的外頭貼上特殊設計的標籤來預付郵資。他的提案被激烈爭論了好幾年。經過認真的討論後，羅蘭・希爾的提案終於獲得採用。1840 年 5 月 6 日，世界上第一張郵票在英國出現了。面值是一便士，上面印有維多利亞女王的頭像。

這張郵票後來稱為「黑便士」，因為它印成黑色。黑便士產生巨大的影響。它改變了通訊世界，就像如今的電子郵件一樣。黑便士推出後，每年有好幾百萬封信件的寄送，因為幾乎每個人都負擔得起。這套郵寄制度的點子太棒了，所以很快便傳遍全世界。沒多久其他國家也起而效尤。1843 年，巴西是世界上第二個使用黏貼性郵票的國家，這種郵票又名「靶心」。1847 年，美國政府正式地發行第一張郵票，上面印著班傑明・富蘭克林的肖像。到了 1860 年，已有九十幾個國家與殖民地發行郵票。

1. 第一個發行郵票的國家是 _____。
   (A) 美國　(B) **英國**　(C) 德國　(D) 巴西
   見第二段倒數第二句與第三段倒數第二句。

2. 世界上最早的郵票是什麼樣子？
   (A) **黑色的郵票，印有維多利亞女王的頭像。**
   (B) 黑白的郵票，印有班傑明・富蘭克林。
   (C) 藍色的郵票，印有牛眼。
   (D) 紅色的郵票，印有伊莉莎白女王的頭像。
   見第二段最後一句和第三段第一句。

3. 下列哪一項有關 1840 年以前郵政制度的敘述是不正確的？
   (A) 寄信的費用非常高。
   (B) 郵資依距離而定。
   (C) **郵差必須很費力地向寄件者收錢。**
   (D) 收件者必須付郵資。
   見第一段第四句。

4. 本文中哪一個字和 "receiver" 同義？
   (A) 改革。　　　　(B) 側面像。
   (C) 寄件者。　　　(D) **收件者。**
   線索在第二段第二句 sender 和 addressee 是相反詞。

5. 本文可以類推出 _____。
   (A) 黑便士也可以在英國的殖民地購得
   (B) 第一枚美國郵票是班傑明・富蘭克林設計的
   (C) **在 1840 年以前英國的郵政服務招致許多民眾的不滿與批評**
   (D) 英國是唯一永遠有女王頭像在郵票上的國家。
   線索在第一段第四、五句提出的困擾，造成後來的改革。

postage n. 郵資	reform n. 改革	addressee n. 收件者
basis n. 基礎	proposal n. 提議	profile n. 側面像
adhesive adj. 黏著的	portrait n. 畫像	colony n. 殖民地

人類最好的朋友學新招
Man's Best Friend Learns a New Trick

最近的研究顯示，狗的嗅覺可能比我們原本所想的還好。研究人員宣稱狗有嗅出癌症的能力。1989 年，醫學期刊《柳葉刀》上的一篇文章報導，有隻狗一直聞著主人腳上的一顆痣，結果發現是皮膚癌。

後來在 2004 年，《英國醫學期刊》刊登了一篇有關狗設法分辨膀胱癌味道的研究。卡洛琳‧威利斯博士 (Carolyn Willis) 與她的團隊在 7 個月期間，訓練 6 隻品種與年齡不同的狗分辨有膀胱癌與無膀胱癌患者的尿液。整體而言，狗從 54 次測試中正確挑出膀胱癌尿液 22 次。

2006 年，加州松樹街基金會所做的新研究顯示，一般家犬只要受過幾週的基本訓練，就學會正確分辨肺癌與乳癌患者及健康受測者的呼吸取樣。邁克‧包夫曼 (Michael Broffman) 與邁克‧麥庫洛奇 (Michael McCulloch) 表示，乳癌樣本的辨識成功率是 88 %，肺癌樣本則是 99 %。

狗的鼻子是被調整到很精準的工具，能分辨比人的鼻子可察覺之氣味弱一千倍的味道。癌細胞成長時會釋放有機物質。即使有機物質的量非常少，狗的嗅覺也足以察覺與辨識到。

既然狗真的可以偵測癌症，未來將會如何呢？有些研究人員認為，狗可以當成醫生診療室裡的「預警系統」，用來偵測病人的癌症。其他研究人員則希望以 Fido 機器鼻做為開發新式「機器鼻」的藍圖，讓機器鼻可以像狗的鼻子一樣運作，但不需要時常散步。

1. 嗅覺是 _____ 的感覺。
  (A) 品嚐　(B) 聞　(C) 聽　(D) 看
  線索在第一段第二句。

2. 下列有關威利斯博士的研究哪一項是正確的？
  (A) 研究在刊登在 2004 年美國的醫學期刊上。
  (B) 6 隻同品種的狗被教導來嗅出膀胱癌病人的尿液。
  (C) 她指出狗可以偵測皮膚癌的特性。
  (D) 在威利斯博士的實驗中狗的成功率大約是百分之 41。
  見第二段第三句。(A)、(C)見第一句；(B)則見第二句。

3. 包夫曼和麥庫洛奇的研究目的是要找出是否 _____。
  (A) 癌症可以從人的呼吸中聞出來
  (B) 狗可以聞得出皮膚腫瘤
  (C) 不同品種的狗有不同的嗅覺能力
  (D) 狗的鼻子要比人類敏銳一千倍
  見第三段第一句。

4. 第四段 "them" 這個代名詞指涉 _____。
  (A) 細胞　(B) 量　(C) 物質　(D) 氣味

5. 本文可以類推出 _____。
  (A) 使用狗來偵測癌症是不實際的
  (B) 科學家希望最後能發展出可以比擬 Fido 機器鼻來偵測癌細胞
  (C) 狗將來能夠聞出血液中的癌細胞。
  (D) 狗將來可以辨認肺癌的期數來幫助人類。
  見最後一段最後一句。

olfactory	adj. 嗅覺的	mole	n. 痣
breed	n. 品種	urine	n. 尿液

bladder　n.　膀胱
blueprint　n.　藍圖

你知道粉紅豹一角是為了某部電影所創作，但實際上並不在影片裡嗎？那部電影是在 1963 年拍攝，名叫《粉紅豹》，內容是關於名貴寶石的竊案及笨拙的法國偵探為了破案所展開的有趣冒險。電影中的「粉紅豹」是鑽石的名稱，內有裂縫。仔細瞧時，裂縫狀似粉紅豹。

電影片商需要為片頭及片尾謝幕表弄點東西，所以決定製作一個簡短的卡通。想當然爾，他們選了一隻粉紅色的卡通豹。電影相當賣座，還拍了好幾部續集。粉紅豹一角深受大眾喜愛。不僅其他的電影也用到他，還製作了以他為主角的短片及長期播放的電視卡通影集。有趣的是，因為卡通並無對白，所以受到國際喜愛。這使得卡通很容易看懂，因為觀眾只需要觀賞劇情發展就行了，而且還伴隨著一樣出名的粉紅豹主題配樂的播放。

粉紅豹在 60 年代末期與 70 年代相當受歡迎。創作者將該角色授權，粉紅豹便開始出現在玩具與各種商品上。他也被用在廣告上，是所有想要販賣粉紅色系商品的公司的最愛。事實上，他是歐文斯・科寧 (Owens Corning) 玻璃纖維絕緣材料的代言人，他們想出令人難忘的口號「Think Pink!」。

雖然粉紅豹不曾真正消失過，但他在 2006 年因為原版電影的重新翻拍而引起更多的注意。大家要忘了他還要很長的時間。你不這樣認為嗎？只要問某個人他們想到「粉紅」時會聯想到什麼就好了。

1. 這顆鑽石被命名為粉紅豹是因為 ＿＿＿＿。
(A) 那是它主人的名字
(B) 它是電影片名

(C) 它裡面的裂縫看起來像粉紅豹
(D) 它是最熱門的卡通人物
見第一段最後一句。

2. 最初的電影主要內容是關於什麼？
(A) 鑽石的品質。　　(B) 鑽石的盜竊。
(C) 冒險的假期。　　(D) 粉紅豹的笨拙。
見第一段第三句。

3. 下列哪一項有關頑皮豹一角的敘述是不正確的？
(A) 有此卡通人物的玩具在 70 年代通過授權出現。
(B) 它最早出現在 1963 年電影的開頭和結尾。
(C) 它直到 70 年代才變得受歡迎。
(D) 它的受歡迎造成電視上卡通影集的出現。
見第三段第一句。

4. 第二段 "this" 這個代名詞指涉 ＿＿＿＿。
(A) 以這人物為特色　(B) 主題音樂
(C) 引起國際的興趣　(D) 沒有說話
線索就在上一句的文意。

5. 由本文可以類推出 ＿＿＿＿。
(A) 粉紅色是歐文斯・科寧玻璃纖維絕緣材料的商標
(B) 2006 年名為粉紅豹的新電影非常賣座
(C) 粉紅豹不會被記得很久
(D) 拍攝過好幾部粉紅豹電影，其中只有兩部的片名有粉紅豹
線索在第三段第四句中的 **the memorable slogan "Think Pink"**。

theft　n.　偷竊
merchandise　n.　商品
flaw　n.　裂縫
fiberglass　n.　玻璃纖維
sequel　n.　續集
insulation　n.　絕緣材料

肯‧凱西 (Ken Kesey)，《飛越杜鵑窩》，潘出版社，1962 年。255 頁。

幾位精神病院病患的規律生活，因為嗓門大、精力旺盛的病患麥梅菲 (R.P. McMurphy) 的出現而大不相同。麥梅菲入院後，我們看到他藉由違背護士長的命令來「反抗制度」。麥梅菲努力讓其他病患反抗護士長，護士長則以欺騙病患及運用威權控制他們的方式予以反擊。這造成一些死亡及某些病患的身心解放。

加布里爾‧賈西亞‧馬奎斯 (Gabriel Garcia Marquez)，《百年孤寂》，哈潑與羅出版社，1970年。383 頁。

《百年孤寂》發生在虛構的馬康多鎮 (Macondo) 裡，描述邦迪亞 (Buendia) 一家的故事。在 7 個世代間，馬康多鎮與邦迪亞家族歷經戰火、侵略與水災。故事主要是採用魔幻寫實風格，這是一種在寫實場景中，發生看似不可能發生的事物的寫作風格，例如動物說話與人類飛天等等。

詹姆斯‧迪基 (James Dickey)，《解救》，戴爾出版社，1970 年。278 頁。

4 個男人決定搭乘小船順著虛構的卡胡拉瓦西河 (Cahulawassee) 而下，這是喬治亞州最大最偏遠的河流。航程一開始雖然平靜，但一切馬上變得很危險，因為他們必須和異常荒野又湍急的河水，及住在森林中的危險人物奮戰。本書獲選為 20 世紀最重要的百大小說之一。

尼克‧宏比 (Nick Hornby)，《非關男孩》，靛藍出版社，1998 年。286 頁。

這個故事是描述一個寂寞且飽受欺負的小男生馬可斯 (Marcus) 與富有、無聊的 36 歲男子威爾 (Will) 之間的友誼。男孩的母親非常奇怪，不瞭解他在學校需要和其他的小孩處得來。威爾對生活沒有任何抱負，靠著老爸賺來的錢維生。2002 年這個故事改編成同名的電影。

1. 以下哪一本書最厚？
　(A) 飛越杜鵑窩。　　**(B) 百年孤寂。**
　(C) 解救。　　　　(D) 非關男孩。
　搜尋每本書的頁數即可得知。

2. 哪一本書在 2002 年拍成電影？
　(A) 飛越杜鵑窩。　　(B) 百年孤寂。
　(C) 解救。　　　　**(D) 非關男孩。**

3. 哪一本書談有關一個家族 7 代的故事？
　(A) 飛越杜鵑窩。　　**(B) 百年孤寂。**
　(C) 解救。　　　　(D) 非關男孩。

4. 誰寫了有關 4 個人在一條河上的冒險旅程？
　(A) 肯‧凱西。
　(B) 加布里爾‧賈西亞‧馬奎斯。
　(C) 詹姆斯‧迪基。
　(D) 尼克‧宏比。

5. 誰寫的書描寫精神病院發生的事？
　(A) 肯‧凱西。
　(B) 加布里爾‧賈西亞‧馬奎斯。
　(C) 詹姆斯‧迪基。
　(D) 尼克‧宏比。

cuckoo	n.	杜鵑	institution	n.	機構
deliverance	n.	解脫	bully	v.	恐嚇

solitude	n.	孤寂
seemingly	adv.	看似

歌唱精神
The Spirit of Singing

　　黑人靈歌有好幾項特色影響了美國音樂的發展。黑人靈歌是 19 世紀初從美國奴隸的音樂衍生出來的，這些奴隸常被迫改信基督教。他們把對新信仰的寄望與非洲傳統歌曲結合在一起，創造出獨特的美國音樂風格。

　　黑人靈歌的一項特色是「呼喊」。大家反覆吟唱著一句歌詞，一邊迅速繞圈跳舞，這是來自非洲宗教的傳統。1930 年代以後，靈歌變成所謂的「福音音樂」，但是很多歌曲中仍然保有一些「呼喊」成分。

　　黑人靈歌的第二項特色是「呼叫與回應」，這是由領唱者唱一句，歌者回下一句。盲人美國歌手雷・查爾斯 (Ray Charles) 以混合音樂風格著稱，他在「What I'd Say」與「Hit the Road Jack」等等非靈歌中運用這種技巧。雖然有些黑人基督教團體的成員對於查爾斯使用「呼叫與回應」提出批評，但是在早期以宏亮歌聲及明快節奏為主的搖滾樂中，這卻變成一項流行的特色。

　　受到靈歌影響的現代重要音樂風格是節奏藍調，又稱為「R&B」。這種音樂對美國有很大的影響。結合福音唱法與爵士樂器及藍調節拍，R&B 在貓王與滾石樂團等搖滾歌手中可以聽到，另外在瑪麗・布萊姬 (Mary J. Blige) 與賈斯汀・提姆布萊克 (Justin Timberlake) 等現代嘻哈歌手身上也可以聽到。

　　雖然黑人靈歌一開始是用來撫慰奴隸，但它們已變成世世代代美國樂手的一大靈感來源。它們的影響力幫忙創造了全球皆知的獨特美式音樂。

1. 本文主要的目的是說明 ＿＿＿＿ 。

(A) 節奏藍調的特色
(B) 黑人靈歌的發展和影響
(C) 搖滾和節奏藍調之間的差異
(D) 黑人靈歌對全世界音樂的影響
本文主要談黑人靈歌的由來和它的影響。

2. 依據本文，下列何者為真？
(A) 黑人靈歌追溯到 19 世紀末期。
(B) 黑人靈歌在美國黑奴被解放時產生。
(C) 黑人靈歌運用領唱者和歌者之間的呼叫與回應技巧。
(D) 福音歌曲對黑人靈歌的發展有很大的影響。
見第三段第一句。

3. 第二段 "chanted" 最適合以 ＿＿＿＿ 取代？
(A) 畫畫　(B) 拉　**(C) 唱**　(D) 保存
線索在 chanted 後面的 a line。

4. 可以由本文類推奴隸創作靈歌是為了要 ＿＿＿＿ 。
(A) 抒發痛苦　　　　(B) 娛樂主人
(C) 表達高昂的情緒 (D) 表達對主人的謝意
線索在最後一段第一句中的 a source of comfort。

5. 哪一項不是黑人靈歌發展的因素？
(A) 奴隸制度的狀態。
(B) 非洲傳統。
(C) 對上帝信念。
(D) 美國印地安傳統。
見第一段第二、三句。

Negro n. 黑人	spiritual n. 靈歌	convert v. 改變信仰
Christianity n. 基督教	chant v. 吟唱	gospel adj. 福音的
tempo n. 速度	beat n. 節拍	inspiration n. 靈感

在當今的時尚業裡，有兩大議題登上全球頭條。其中一個攸關人命，另一個則攸關動物的生命。

從 1960 年代開始，時尚圈越來越要求模特兒必須要非常纖瘦。這種「纖瘦就是成功」的想法讓很多模特兒都有飲食失調的問題。評論家也認為很多易受影響的少女會檢視纖瘦模特兒的相片，然後意圖讓自己看起來一樣。他們說這已經使得少女罹患厭食症與暴食症之類的飲食疾病比例增加。

最近，在時尚業終於看到些微的變化。2006年，馬德里時尚週禁止所有過瘦的模特兒走伸展台。籌辦者表示他們這麼做是為了向少女提倡更健康的形象。不過，大多數的設計師還是偏好最瘦的模特兒，即便最近一位超級名模露西爾・雷莫斯 (Luisel Ramos) 才剛死於厭食症。

時尚業面臨的第二個重要議題是在衣物上使用動物皮草。反皮草慈善組織「InFURmation」表示，每年有五千萬以上的動物因為他們的毛皮而喪命，其中最受歡迎的選擇是狐狸、兔子與狼。有些頂尖時尚設計者，例如凱文・克萊 (Calvin Klein) 與傑・邁凱羅 (Jay McCarroll)，已經禁止在他們的作品中使用皮草。可悲的是，2006 與 2007 年，對皮草的使用興趣再起，時尚店內又出現皮草衣物。

有些人爭論說人們對於自己的體重及衣服的質料都應該能夠自己選擇。不過時尚業在有能力影響大眾的看法之下，當然應該負責提倡好的原則。如果體重合宜的模特兒穿非皮草製品，世界一定會充滿更健康、更快樂的年輕女性及更健康、更快樂的動物。

1. 本文主要是關於 _____ 。
   (A) 超瘦的模特兒和飲食疾病
   (B) 飲食疾病和時裝設計師
   (C) **超瘦的模特兒和皮草的使用**
   (D) 時裝設計師和皮草的使用
   本文第二和第四段引言提到這兩項議題。

2. 馬德里時尚週禁止超瘦模特兒的目的是 _____ 。
   (A) 製造頭條新聞。
   (B) 訂立一個新的時裝趨勢
   (C) **展現更健康的身體形象**
   (D) 促銷時裝產品
   見第三段第三句。

3. "InFURmation" 這個機構可能是努力於 _____ 。
   (A) 禁止超瘦模特兒走伸展台
   (B) **阻止人們殺動物取其皮毛**
   (C) 幫助得厭食症的少女
   (D) 保護狐狸和狼這類的野生動物
   由第四段的敘述推斷。

4. 依據本文，下列何者不正確？
   (A) 自從 1960 年代以來，人們一直都喜愛很瘦的模特兒。
   (B) 超瘦的伸展台模特兒對少女有負面影響。
   (C) 凱文・克萊不再在他的作品中使用皮毛。
   (D) **多數設計師跟隨馬德里禁用超瘦模特兒。**
   見第三段最後一句。

5. 作者對這兩項禁令的態度為何？
   (A) **贊成。**　(B) 反對。　(C) 中立。　(D) 冷淡。
   見最後一段二、三句。

issue	n.	議題	vulnerable	adj.	易受影響的
bulimia	n.	暴食症	ban	v.	禁止

anorexia　n.　厭食症
catwalk　n.　伸展台

　　現代科學讓人可以從一顆藥丸裡獲得所需的一切維生素。美國人每年花兩百三十億美元購買合成維他命。不過，這些合成的營養素和由食物攝取的天然維生素一樣健康嗎？

　　對於合成維他命的主要憂慮是，很多國家並未嚴格加以規範。例如，美國政府要求製造合成維他命的公司在罐裝標示上列出成分，卻不檢測這些聲明或處罰違法者。公司也可以謊報維他命的成分。例如，有些維他命被發現鉛含量太多，可能導致嚴重疾病。此外，有些合成維他命實際上不含他們宣稱的營養素含量。這表示服用這些藥丸的人所攝取的維生素並沒有他們想得那麼多。

　　相反的，真正的食物可以提供人很多天然的維生素，卻沒有合成維他命所帶來的風險。人們如果吃包含許多蔬果的均衡飲食，就會吸收到健康生活所需的一切維生素。人們應該試著只吃天然食物，盡可能避免加工食品。另外攝取多元的食物也很重要。這樣就可以確定他們從多種不同的來源獲得許多種類的維生素。

　　合成維他命雖然方便，但不可以靠它們獲取膳食需要。相反的，人們可以改由天然食物獲得維生素，這是過長壽、健康生活的最佳方式。

1. 作者對合成維他命的態度為何？
　(A) 正面的。　　　　**(B) 負面的。**
　(C) 中立的。　　　　(D) 冷淡的。
　見最後一段。

2. 第二段 "regulate" 的字義是 _____。
　(A) 以獎品來鼓勵
　(B) 以正常方式處理
　(C) 藉由法律或規則來控制
　(D) 以嚴格的方式處理
　線索在下一句 (rules)。

3. 作者提到「公司也可以謊報維他命的成分」的目的是什麼？
　(A) 說明公司如何獲利。
　(B) 說明為什麼合成維他命在人體是無用的。
　(C) 比較製造出來的成分和聲稱的成分之份量。
　(D) 討論服用合成維他命所冒的風險。
　線索在下兩句所提出來的例子。

4. 依據本文，下列何者為非？
　(A) 天然維生素取自真正的食物。
　(B) 有些合成維他命被發現含有有害的礦物質。
　(C) 均衡的飲食供給我們所需的天然維生素。
　(D) 美國人年年花數百萬美元在合成維他命上。
　見第一段第二句。

5. 第二段 "they" 這個代名詞指涉 _____。
　(A) 成分
　(B) 人
　(C) 一些合成維他命
　(D) 營養物

---

synthetic	adj.	合成的	nutrient	n.	營養素	regulate	v.	規範
ingredient	n.	成分	dietary	adj.	飲食的	requirement	n.	需要

購物狂是指對購物上癮的人。他們大多在日常生活中經歷挫敗或憂鬱。對他們來說，購物是這些負面感受的暫時逃避。最近柯蘭 (Koran) 博士所做的研究顯示，美國人口中約有 6 ％屬於這個族群——比美國有賭癮的人還多，而且不分男女。

有些社會情況也是造成購物狂現象的原因。信用卡的容易取得鼓勵大家先消費，稍後再擔心財務責任。網路與電視購物頻道也讓購物變得更容易。大眾文化是另一個因素。在雜誌或《購物狂》系列書籍與《慾望城市》之類的電視節目薰陶下，購物已經變成生活的一種需求。

購物對這些人來說還衍生出額外的問題。他們過於沈迷購物，以致於沒有足夠的時間與親朋好友共處。這可能損及他們的關係。再者，過度刷卡也常導致他們債台高築。鉅額債務所引起的不安可能導致他們更加憂鬱。

心理學家建議他們面對現實。購物狂應該坦承他們不顧一切的購物行為意謂著生活失序。了解這點後，他們可以開始面對，而不是逃避真正煩擾他們的事情。一些美國心理學家已經開設戒癮課程。購物狂被教導如何控制購物習慣。例如，教他們停卡，只用現金購物。也鼓勵他們在突然覺得需要購物時就去做其他的活動。

1. 本文中未提到以下哪一個導致購物癮的因素？
   (A) 心理因素。　　(B) 社會因素。
   (C) 文化因素。　　(D) 生物因素。
   一、二段中未提到(D)選項。

2. 本文中未提到以下哪一個購物癮造成的問題？
   (A) 財務問題。　　(B) 職業問題。
   (C) 心理問題。　　(D) 人際關係問題。
   第三段三、四、五句分別提到家人和朋友間的關係、債務與憂鬱。

3. 第四段 "confront" 最適合以 _____ 替代？
   (A) 誘捕　　　　　(B) 逃避
   (C) 面對　　　　　(D) 欺騙
   線索在後面的 **rather than run away from**。

4. 戒癮課程設計來 _____ 。
   (A) 使用藥物治療購物狂
   (B) 提供購物狂行為治療
   (C) 教導購物狂如控制毒癮
   (D) 幫助購物狂學習如何用信用卡購物
   見最後一段第五句。

5. 依據本文，下列何者為非？
   (A) 有些購物狂用購物當作解決憂鬱的方法。
   (B) 因為有網路和電視購物節目，購物變得更容易。
   (C) 男人和女人一樣可能變成購物狂。
   (D) 在美國，有賭癮的人比有購物癮的人多。
   見第一段最後一句。

shopaholic	n.	購物狂	addicted	adj.	上癮的
phenomenon	n.	現象	excessive	adj.	過度的
reckless	adj.	不顧一切的	confront	v.	面對

outnumber	v.	數目比…多
overwhelming	adj.	壓倒性的

紐約，12 月 5 日──紐約市衛生局全體一致通過全球第一個在餐廳幾乎完全禁用反式脂肪的規定。

衛生局委員湯瑪斯・費萊頓博士 (Thomas R. Frieden) 表示，這項禁令是回應市民希望餐廳食物不要使用有害的反式脂肪。店家有 18 個月的時間用較健康的選擇取代反式脂肪。之後，每份食物的反式脂肪含量不得超過 0.5 公克。

反式脂肪發明於 20 世紀初。在植物油中加入氫所製成，1970 年代反式脂肪受到食品製造商的青睞，以它來取代有害的飽和性脂肪。餐廳老闆偏好反式脂肪，因為它們的保存期限較長，讓食物更香脆。

市政府表示，餐廳的食物不使用反式脂肪可以拯救生命。人造的反式脂肪會提高血液中的壞膽固醇，降低好膽固醇。醫學研究發現，食用反式脂肪會增加心臟病、中風與早逝的風險。

健康專家與市民都支持這項禁令，醫學團體也表示完全支持。市長邁克・彭博 (Michael R. Bloomberg) 也為此決定辯護。他說：「沒人想拿走你的薯條與漢堡」，但強調這些食物應該做得更健康。

不過，商業團體反對這項禁令。全國餐飲協會的發言人唐恩・弗萊舍 (Dan Fleischer) 表示，這是用法律規範健康的「錯誤嘗試」。餐廳業者也表示憂心。他們說禁令會讓他們營運困難，不過慶幸還有 18 個月可以尋找烹調食物的其他方法。

1. 食用反式脂肪會 _____ 而增加心臟病的風險。
   (A) **增加壞膽固醇並且降低好膽固醇**
   (B) 對人的情緒造成負面的影響
   (C) 降低人吃進的食物的營養程度
   (D) 增加人的壓力程度和影響血糖
   見第四段第二句。

2. 依據本文，餐廳使用反式脂肪是為了它的 _____。
   (A) 風味和低價
   (B) **貯存壽命和不同的風味**
   (C) 高營養成分和口味
   (D) 低價和方便性
   見第三段最後一句。

3. 依據本文，下列何者不實？
   (A) 大多數的紐約市民支持這項禁令。
   (B) 衛生局給商家 18 個月換掉反式脂肪。
   (C) **反式脂肪是將氫加入動物油中製造出來的。**
   (D) 反式脂肪直到 1970 年代開始受到食品公司的歡迎。
   見第三段第二句。

4. 下列何者可能是費萊頓博士會說的？
   (A) 「彭博市長只是想要上頭條新聞。」
   (B) 「反式脂肪不會對心臟健康造成那麼負面的影響。」
   (C) **「反式脂肪消失後，沒有人會懷念它的。」**
   (D) 「紐約市無權立法管制健康。」
   第二段第一句得知費萊頓博士支持禁令。四個選項只有(C)是支持者的話。

5. 由本文可以類推出 _____。
   (A) 紐約速食的價格將會上漲
   (B) 紐約人將會吃更多薯條和漢堡
   (C) 其他城市將跟隨紐約市認可相同的禁令
   (D) **食品公司正在找尋或研發新的油來替代反式脂肪**
   見本文最後一句。

trans fat 反式脂肪	unanimously adv. 一致地	commissioner n. 委員
hydrogen n. 氫	saturated adj. 飽和的	crispy adj. 酥脆的
cholesterol n. 膽固醇	premature death 早逝	legislate v. 立法規定

關於 Reading Power

這是一套為愉閱英語而生，

一套能體驗英閱樂趣，

完全閱讀導引　精采內容

★ 第一部份為理論篇，分析閱讀測驗出題方向與作答技巧，幫助您打好根基。

★ 第二部分精選四十篇主題多元、趣味 與知識 兼具的文章，幫助您進行閱讀測驗的實戰練習。

★ 文章用字符合大考中心公佈的高中英文參考詞彙表第一～四級範圍，且配合全民英檢中級程度。

★ 適用於高中職學生升學準備或一般讀者強化閱讀能力。

一套能開拓視野見聞，

一套能厚植英語實力，

一套讓人愛不釋手的系列叢書。

「完全閱讀導引」與「翻譯與解析」不分售